COSMIC SABOTEUR

By
FRANK M. ROBINSON

ARMCHAIR FICTION
PO Box 4369, Medford, Oregon   97501-0168

*For more information about Armchair Books and products, visit our
website at…*

www.armchairfiction.com

Or email us at…

armchairfiction@yahoo.com

THE ULTIMATE TRAITOR TO EARTH!

They told him that he hated the Earth, beating him until he nearly died—for he must be convinced! But it was all part of his wicked indoctrination as a Cosmic Saboteur. But hanging in the balance was the future of his own people—and his own planet. For if the Thuscans had their way, every major city on Earth would eventually become a smoking ruin, paving the path for an alien takeover and the end of mankind.

Veteran sci-fi author Frank M. Robinson spins a taut tale of futuristic espionage, intrigue, and betrayal in this fine novel of a planet on the verge of total destruction.

FOR A COMPLETE SECOND NOVEL, TURN TO PAGE 91

CAST OF CHARACTERS

STANLEY MARTIN
A smart kid from Chicago, just out for a walk one day when his life came crashing down and the fate of Earth fell into his hands.

FRED TANNER
Dressed in a suit, sometimes a smile on his face, but always ready to torture or murder—something he enjoyed immensely.

AVIS
Stanley knew one thing for sure, he must kill this hard-looking yet beautiful woman. But there was something about her...

MR. MALCOM
He seemed to be calm and very business-like, but he wouldn't hesitate to order brutal punishment...or perhaps even worse.

MR. AINSWORTH
In a nightmarish world of torture, he looked to be the only friend Stanley Martin had—but sometimes looks can be deceiving.

ELAL
Just because you're the leader of a space fleet doesn't mean you have the courage to lead it.

CHAPTER ONE

THEY jumped him when he was walking past an alley, a couple of blocks from the stockyards on Chicago's brawling South Side.

He had gotten off the "El" two stops down because it was a damn fine Spring morning and he liked to walk through the Polish section and watch the city wake up. He was 17 years old and he hadn't grown cynical with the world yet. He liked the clean, fresh smell of the early morning and he got a kick out of the sleepy-eyed housewives in their ratty bathrobes, banging open the front door to bring in the milk and the morning paper.

He'd pick up the live-stock reports, he thought, hop an "El" back uptown and maybe he'd be at Amalgamated News Service only a couple of minutes late. And if they didn't like it, they knew what they could do about it. His kid brother ran copy at the News and he said they could use another boy down there.

"Stan," Larry had said, *"you're wasting your time at AMS. You won't get as much dough at the News but you'll learn something."*

Which was something to consider because Larry was one bright cookie and someday he was really going to be somebody...

It was early morning and nobody had started to work yet—the streets were deserted. There was a chill in the air and he stopped by an open alley to light a weed and take the clamminess out of his lungs.

And then he got it.

A handful of knuckles right in the mouth, splintering his teeth and splitting his lip so he sprayed blood like somebody had squeezed a sponge. It was hard to get a good look because the shock had filled his eyes with tears. But there were three of them and they were grown men—and the biggest he had seen outside of a television wrestling match.

He screamed *"Help!"* just once before a hand as big as a typewriter buried itself wrist deep in his stomach. He doubled up and went limp, gasping for breath. One of the men caught him by the jacket collar and pulled him further into the alley, to the back of a restaurant where there was a small mountain of empty boxes and garbage cans full of orange peels and eggshells and stale doughnuts.

Nobody said a word.

He was still fighting for his breath and feeling sick when they stood him up against the refuse pile and started going over him scientifically, cutting his face and hitting him in the kidneys. He tried to blink away the blood that kept streaming into his eyes, to get a good look at them. But they kept working on his face until all the world was a bloody haze and it was hard to even make out light and shadow…

He lashed out once and heard a satisfying grunt and then somebody hit his wrists with a slat of wood, deadening the nerves so he couldn't close his hands. He tried to scream but he had no wind left and he realized dimly it wouldn't have done much good. The streets were deserted and it was the type of neighborhood where nobody went to anybody else's rescue—least of all, early in the morning.

A fist caught him flush on the side of the jaw and he staggered over against the garbage cans and fell to the bricks, his face half buried in the stinking garbage. He played dead dog for a moment, catching his breath, then scrambled to his knees, clawing handfuls of rotting orange peels and decayed bones to throw at the three silent men in front of him.

"You'll never get away with this! The cops…"

The toe of a shoe caught him in the groin and he collapsed again. He didn't even recognize the thin screaming that sounded in his ears as his own.

A voice from a million miles away said, *"We're not supposed to kill him!"* And he guessed that the men were from out of town because it was an accent that he had never heard before. Then two of them were holding him up, twisting his arms behind him, while the third stuffed garbage in his mouth, choking him so his screams died away to a dull, muffled sob.

They let him go for a minute and he tried to run away. They laughed and tripped him before he had taken three steps. Then they jerked him to his feet and started hitting him again, working him over professionally, chopping at him with fists covered by thin, leather gloves that cut his face and ripped his shirt and jacket.

When he finally slipped limply to the pavement, they let him lay there, kicking him in the thighs and the buttocks. His cap was a dozen feet away, the remnants of his jacket not too far from that. His pants were ripped and his shirt was in shreds, the strips waving like bloody banners in the slight, morning breeze.

One of the three said, *"I guess it's time to go."* Stan could hear running feet and then there was a long silence. He couldn't tell if it was a minute or half an hour later when footsteps again sounded across the bricks and somebody knelt by his side.

"You're hurt, son! Let me help you…"

The voice was soft and full of compassion, like a minister's might be. The man helped him to his feet and Stan lurched to the street and sat down on the curbstone. He tried to wipe away the blood with a tattered shirtsleeve but it still seemed to be running down his cheeks. Then he realized that he was crying.

"Try this."

He felt something pressed into his hands and wiped at his face with the handkerchief.

"T—thanks."

"Who were they, son?"

"I don't know. I was just walking past the alley and they...jumped me. I don't know why. Honest to God, Mister, I don't know why!"

He felt close to crying again and shut up for a moment to try and control the convulsive heaving of his chest. Then he looked up at the man standing next to him.

Black shoes, brand new. Neatly pressed gabardines. Tall and somewhat thin. Wearing a light, black topcoat like you might imagine a priest would wear. A tan hat, also brand new. Middle twenties, with the face of a saint. The face of a man you knew you could trust.

"What's your name, son?"

"Stan. Stanley Martin." He was still close to sobbing and the name came out with too many syllables.

The man pondered for a moment and Stan thought he looked a little like a high school principal trying to guess how bright a student might be.

"We'll have to fix you up, Stan. Then we'll have to take you home." He helped Stan to his feet and guided him over to a black car a few yards down the street.

Far away, there was the wail of a siren.

"The cops," Stan said, hanging back. "I gotta tell the cops."

"There'll be time enough for that later," the man said smoothly. There was the faintest suggestion of haste in his voice.

"I oughta wait," Stan mumbled, but the man pushed him gently into the car and Stan didn't argue. He lay down on the back seat, resting his throbbing head against the cushions and the side of the car. It was a big car, he thought vaguely. Like a rich man's sedan, with a glass partition between the driver and the passengers.

He heard a hissing sound from somewhere and the world started to gray out. And then he suddenly wondered how he could be taken home if the man didn't know where he lived...

Just before he blacked out altogether, a voice said:

"I'm your friend, Stan. Say it to yourself and say it over and over. I'm your friend. I saved your life."

"You're my friend," Stan repeated dully, his mind slipping slowly into a pool of throbbing blackness. "You saved my life..."

The last thing he saw was a quick glimpse of the city streets, the slowly rotting houses, and the bright splashes of green in the front lawns and the cottonwood trees.

CHAPTER TWO

HIS muscles were aching and sore and he felt sick to his stomach.

His eyes wouldn't focus at first and he stayed flat on his mattress and stared at the hazy outlines of the room. It was a funny kind of hospital. Nobody had bandaged his cuts—they were still caked with blood—and he still had on the same torn clothes that smelled of sweat and dirt.

Where had the man taken him?

He shook his head, trying to make out the details of the room, and his vision cleared a little.

The room didn't even come close to a hospital. It was more like a jail. There was the cot that he was sitting on and the washbasin and the flush bowl and the barred door at the entrance. Nothing else. No windows, no desk, no calendar, nothing. Just a small cell of gray, featureless metal.

He stood up, holding on to the cot for support, and touched the bars wonderingly. He hadn't done anything wrong, he thought. Not a damn thing!

"Guard! Guard!"

He'd get a lawyer! Larry had connections and maybe…

There were footsteps outside the cell door and a moment later it swung open. The man who opened it wasn't a guard—at least he didn't dress like one, Stan thought. Just a man in a blue suit. Smiling and urbane and what the ad writers would call dapper.

Except for his eyes. The same kind of cold eyes that an executioner might have. Eyes that had watched people die—slowly.

Stan shivered.

Death. In a blue serge suit.

"I was wondering when you were going to wake up," the man said pleasantly. He held out his hand. "My name's Fred Tanner. You…"

Stan didn't take the hand. "I want to know what's coming off here! Where's the joker who brought me here? Where's…"

"Somebody else can tell you all you want to know," the man said easily. "Just follow me."

Stan didn't move.

"You coming?"

It wasn't a question, it was a statement. Tanner stood there, his head half cocked, watching Stan curiously, like somebody might watch an ant or a bird. Stan started to say something but the words died in his throat. Tanner was no weakling. He had thick wrists and a bull neck and a feeling of power that he wore like a suit of clothes.

He was the type, Stan thought coldly, who could break you in two if he wanted.

He shrugged and followed Tanner down the corridor for a hundred feet and then into a room about the size of his own cell. There was an oval shaped desk in one corner and a tubular chair by it, both of the same metal as the walls and the floor. The whole assembly looked like it had been punched out of one sheet.

The man behind the desk looked like an ex-football player ten years later, Stan thought. A husky man, just starting to go to fat, with thick lips and thinning hair.

Tanner pushed Stan forward. "Here's the boy, Mr. Malcolm."

Stan wet his lips. "I...I'd like to know what this is all about, sir."

"Fred," the man behind the desk said in a bored voice. "He lacks manners."

Tanner casually lashed out, with the flat of his hand and caught Stan on the side of the head—hard. Stan staggered against the wall and half-slid to the floor. He could feel the tears start again.

"Hey! What's the..."

"Again, Fred."

Stan crumpled to the floor, shook his head, and struggled back to his feet. He was dazed but he knew enough not to say anything.

"What's your name?"

"Stanley Martin. I told..."

"Fred."

The blow rocked him but he managed to keep his feet. His legs felt like water.

"How many of your family are living, Martin?"

"Just my mother." He licked his cracked lips. "And my brother. That's all."

"You've lived in Chicago all your life?"

"Yes...yes, sir."

MR. MALCOM finally put down the reports he had been reading and looked up at him. If Tanner's eyes had been cold, Stan thought, then Mr. Malcolm's eyes were frozen.

"You don't like Chicago, do you?"

"I...I guess I like it well enough."

"No, you don't," Mr. Malcolm said smoothly. "You told the other copy boys you hated the city and as soon as you could, you were going to leave it."

Stan gaped. "How did you know?"

"We know a lot of things." Mr. Malcolm leaned casually back in his chair, inspecting Stan like he would a butterfly on a pin. "We know that you hate your mother. And your brother."

"Where do you get that stuff?" Stan bleated, his voice rising. "What are you trying to prove?"

"Fred. Again."

Tanner had to help Stan up.

"I'm going to be sick," Stan said faintly.

The man behind the desk ignored him. "Your mother used to take a strap to you when you came home late, Martin. She used to accuse you of stealing in the stores."

Lies, Stan thought. But he didn't dare talk back.

"Your brother, Larry. He was always your mother's favorite, wasn't he? She always did a lot of things for him that she never did for you, didn't she?"

"Larry never...!"

"Fred."

"I'm sick," Stan whimpered. *"Honest to God, I'm sick!"*

"You hate the city," Mr. Malcolm repeated coldly. "You hate your family."

"I think you're crazy," Stan said weakly. "I want a lawyer."

Mr. Malcolm turned back to his reports.

"Take him to the other cell, Fred."

Back to a cell, Stan thought weakly, following Tanner out. Where at least he could lie down…

But the other cell was too small to lie down in. It measured two feet square and there was no room to lie down. Or even sit down. The most he could do was lean.

He touched the wall with his hand and screamed with pain. The walls were wired for electricity, a thin strip of insulation separating them from the floor. He couldn't lie down, he thought. He didn't have room to sit down and he couldn't even lean against the walls. The only thing he could do was stand up…and stand still.

They took him out eight hours later, when he was too hoarse to scream and the electric walls had no effect on his sagging body.

IT was a different room, this time. A comfortable room with carpets on the floor and pictures on the wall and an over-stuffed sofa of some plastic material along one side.

The man waiting for him was the same young, saintly faced man who had picked him up on the street.

"This is Mr. Ainsworth," Tanner said in a low voice, and nudged him forward.

Mr. Ainsworth looked at him, shocked. "My God, son, haven't they taken care of your cuts?"

Stan just stared at him. Mr. Ainsworth's shocked look faded into one of grim efficiency.

"We'll have to do something about that, son—and right away!" He pressed a button and turned to Tanner. "Take this man to the infirmary immediately, Fred! And don't bring him back here until he's been bathed and issued new clothes!"

He looked back at Stan, his face a study in sympathy and pity. "Believe me, I had no idea…"

It was a reprieve from hell.

He was taken to an infirmary where doctors and nurses, their faces entirely hidden behind gauze masks, bathed him and washed his cuts and covered them with collodion and gave him a hypodermic shot of something that relaxed his muscles and banished his pain completely. They destroyed the rags he had on and in their place he was issued a suit of blue serge, like the one Tanner wore.

When he went back to the room with the carpets and the sofa, Mr. Ainsworth had set up a small dinner table. The room was thick with the fragrance of fried eggs and bacon and hot buttered toast and steaming coffee.

Stan's stomach knotted and turned and he suddenly was sick.

"Take it easy," Mr. Ainsworth said gently. "Go slow at first."

Stan pulled a chair over to the table. He felt weak. Eggs and bacon and coffee…After he had finished, he sat back and took the cigarette that Mr. Ainsworth offered him.

"What am I doing here, Mr. Ainsworth? Why can't I get a lawyer?"

"I wish I could answer all your questions," the saintly-faced man said thoughtfully. "But you have to understand that I'm just a hired hand here. There are some things I'm not at liberty to tell you."

"If I'm not in jail, then just where the hell am I?" Stan asked bitterly.

Mr. Ainsworth held up his hands. "I'm sorry, Stan."

Things weren't adding up, Stan thought, confused. Where was he if he wasn't in jail? The cell and the slightly curving corridor, all of metal. And the doctors and the nurses, their faces almost hidden behind their gauze masks…

"They took me to see a Mr. Malcolm the other day," Stan said in a low voice. "He told me I hated the city and that I even hated my own mother and brother. Can you beat that? Honest, this character…"

His voice trailed away. Mr. Ainsworth was staring at the floor, a frown on his face.

"Everybody builds up resentments against parents who are overly strict, Stan. And it's not unusual for a mother to favor one of her children over the others."

Stan stared at him, open-mouthed.

"But you're agreeing with Mr. Malcolm," he whispered. "Honest, you must be a little crazy, too."

Mr. Ainsworth looked hurt.

"I'm your friend, Stan—I wouldn't lie to you. I didn't save your life just so I could tell you lies."

It was crazy, Stan thought. He had been on his way to the stockyards one morning and the roof had fallen in. He had been kidnapped and tortured apparently for no other reason than to be told he hated his family.

It didn't make sense.

He dropped his cigarette on the carpet and ground it out under his heel. "You're just as bad as the others—you're working right in with them!"

Mr. Ainsworth looked disappointed and pressed a button on his desk. Tanner appeared in the doorway, his face as impersonal as ever.

"You'll have to take him back, Fred." He looked at Stan sadly. "We're trying to be your friends, son, and you won't let us. We're only telling you the truth."

Stan started to shake. "You can go to hell," he blurted.

Tanner took him by the arm to lead him out and the very touch of his hand made Stan tremble even more. He was shaking like a leaf, and he couldn't stop it. It had been such an odd thing. When he had told Mr. Ainsworth he was as bad as the others, Mr. Ainsworth had…flickered.

CHAPTER THREE

THEY stripped him and put him in a room that felt like the inside of a packinghouse refrigerator. His breath came in little wisps of fog and if he stood in one place too long, his feet started to freeze to the floor. He had to keep moving to keep warm and he realized he couldn't keep moving forever. It was cold and damp and at periodic intervals, it rained from pipes overhead. Water that quickly froze on the floor and made his hair a mass of frosted crystals and then started to freeze on him.

He only lasted four hours in the cold room. When they took him out, his nails were broken from clawing at the doorframe and he had started to bleed at the fingertips.

Mr. Malcolm questioned him again.

Why wouldn't he admit that he hated his family? His mother was responsible for his father deserting the family. And his brother used to squeal on him when he was small and had even taken money that Stan used to leave on the dresser.

Stan made the mistake of laughing and ended up in a cell where he couldn't stand, where he had to remain stooped all the time. A small tray of slops appeared after each time he slept and once every sleeping period, somebody cleaned it out.

Mr. Ainsworth questioned him next and it meant a bath and food and cigarettes and rest. He took them and enjoyed them.

Then he told Mr. Ainsworth what he thought of him. They threw him in a small, pitch-black cell and left him there. For weeks. Months.

He spent his time huddled in a corner, thinking of the city and his mother and Larry and what Spring looked like and how leaves that ended up in the Fall as large as your hand, started out as nothing more than a strip of green no bigger than his fingernail. A dozen times a period, he went over the last scene his eyes had glimpsed from Mr. Ainsworth's car. The drab houses and the green trees and the tiny stretch of blue beyond…

And then there were the days when he didn't think of any thing—though he was to wonder later if it had been days or weeks or even only hours. There was nothing by which to judge time, though he tried to keep track of his own pulse and counted the beats into minutes and the minutes into hours and the hours into days.

It was Mr. Ainsworth who rescued him.

"It's been a long time since I've seen you, son."

"You know where I've been."

"Don't hate me, Stan. I'm only trying to help you."

"I appreciate it," Stan said dryly.

And the odd thing was, he honestly *did* appreciate it. Ainsworth represented sleep and a bath and food and clean clothes. And he was grateful. Like any dog that had been kicked and starved and then wagged its tail when it was patted on the head.

And knowing all of this didn't change his reactions in the least.

"Stan," Mr. Ainsworth said quietly, "they want you to say that you hate your family. You say you don't. Perhaps you believe that. But would it hurt to merely say that you do? You don't have to actually believe it." He paused. "And to be perfectly truthful, I'm afraid that you might not live very much longer if you're not willing to go—that far."

Stan jerked, as if somebody had jabbed him with a pin. To come so near to dying so many times had made life seem infinitely precious.

And what did it matter, actually? Some of the things they had been telling him—they weren't exactly lies.

"All right," he said dully. "So I hate the city. And I hate my folks."

Somewhere in his mind, a keystone crumbled.

"That's the way, son. Play it smart!" Mr. Ainsworth looked very proud of himself, as if Stan had just passed a difficult test.

"It's not supposed to stop there, is it?" Stan asked. "What am I supposed to believe in next, so you people won't kill me?"

"I don't think you're looking at it in the right light," Mr. Ainsworth said coldly, and Stan was panic-stricken for fear he would call in Fred and have him taken back to the cold room or the small cell. "We're just telling you things about yourself that you didn't know before."

"Sure," Stan said quickly, trying to sound sincere. "You're just telling me things I never would have suspected."

He got better treatment after that. They assigned him to a cell where he could lie down and sleep and when they talked to him, they offered him cigarettes and joked with him. Even Mr. Malcolm went out of his way to be pleasant. They were uncannily accurate when they told him about his past life and he got to thinking more and more that there was something in what they said.

His mother had been no prize and his brother was a lying, little sneak.

Almost a year went by before they led him up to the big one.

When they told him, point blank, that he hated humanity.

STAN felt like somebody had knocked the wind out of him. "You can't be serious!"

Mr. Ainsworth sighed and shook his head. "Stan, do you remember when I first picked you up? Three of your fellow human beings had dragged you into an alley and were beating you up—you would have been killed if I hadn't come along." He shrugged. "That's the human race for you, son."

"But they were only three individuals!" Stan objected.

"And the others are so much different?" Mr. Ainsworth sneered. "Nobody cared about you, Stan—not even your own family. No human being cares for anybody else but himself! There's a war in every generation where they slaughter each other by the millions. And sickness. Have they ever made any really concerted drive against it? Have they ever really tried to stamp out poverty?"

His lip curled. "They're apes. Nothing but apes!"

"You talk like you're not human," Stan said, and then realized that he had made a mistake.

Mr. Ainsworth started to flicker again, like film in a projector that's run down. Stan gripped the sides of his chair and froze, trying desperately not to show his fear.

Mr. Ainsworth was watching him closely. "I think we should tell you what this is all about, Stan. Watch."

He pressed a button on his desk and the wall behind him started to glow, then drifted away like cigarette smoke. Stan closed his eyes, feeling dizzy and sick and horribly afraid that he was going to fall. He opened them again, slowly.

The end of the room opened out on a harsh, black sky dusted with the tiny pinpoints of stars. Stars that didn't twinkle but shone with a bright, steady blaze. To his left and below he could see a huge segment of a mottled green and blue globe, laced over with shifting shreds of white.

He was almost sick again and then the grandeur of the scene struck him and he caught his breath, sharply.

He was somewhere in space, suspended thousands of miles above his home planet and seeing the universe as man had never seen it before. The blazing infinity of stars and the slowly rolling, green globe that was the Earth...

"The home of the apes," Mr. Ainsworth mused. He paused. "We can use that planet to far better advantage than the human race. We intend to take it. And you're going to help us."

Stan looked at Mr. Ainsworth coldly.

"What's in it for me?"

CHAPTER FOUR

"HALF the world," Mr. Ainsworth said slowly. "One half of your whole, wide world..."

Stan stared at him coldly for a full minute, then started to laugh—laughter then ripped out of him like waves and washed against the sides of the room.

Sick laughter, because he knew the price he was going to have to pay for it.

He sobered. There was a time, he thought, when every human being had to stand up and be counted as a brave man or a coward. This was his.

"And you thought I would take it? You thought I would sell out the whole human race?" His face was seamed with hate and he thumped his chest proudly, suddenly not caring what happened to himself. His voice was hoarse. "I'm one of the apes, remember? They're *my* people and it's *my* planet..."

Mr. Ainsworth's face looked like it was carved from a block of ice.

"Look at me, Martin. *Look at me!*"

Stan looked and felt the sweat pop out on his forehead and his stomach knot into a small, hard ball.

Mr. Ainsworth was fading, the frames slipping past so slow Stan could count them. And the image that was building up in Mr. Ainsworth's place...

Stan screamed and staggered back against the bulkhead, his arm raised before his eyes.

"You're going to help us," the creature said in a horribly liquid voice. *"You're going to help us because you want to. We need advance men to soften this planet up. You're going to be one of them... And after you've done your work, our fleet will arrive!"*

It paused dryly.

"But I see you've still got some indoctrination to go through..."

They took him back to one of the cells and starved him and let him live in his own filth until he wasn't sure if he was a human being or some sort of animal. They made him horribly afraid of pain until he screamed in agony when they merely laid the knives on the table. And with pain as a wedge, they took his personality apart piece by piece and flayed it and tortured it until it no longer resembled the personality that had once been Stanley Martin.

He was cut off from all contact with human beings—or creatures who had masqueraded as human. Tanner had disappeared and Mr. Ainsworth and Mr. Malcolm no longer bothered to appear as Homo sapiens. They saw him every waking day and if their interviews had been harsh before, now they were brutal beyond belief.

He believed what they said and he thought what they wanted him to think.

Not to have done so would have meant death.

But there was still...resistance.

The personality that had been Stanley Martin wasn't entirely gone. There were still shattered fragments of memories and wishes and desires that hadn't been entirely obliterated. Tiny fragments that made him unreliable.

ON the last day, he was strapped into a machine with clamps that fastened tightly to his head and chest.

The lights dimmed and he was alone in the darkness.

"What is your name?"

The tiny fragments of personality struggled and thought and then collapsed in bewilderment.

"I...I'm not sure."

The voices from nowhere continued.

"You have a family. You hate that family."

A faint, drifting haze of memories. Of a woman who had cooked his meals and tucked him into bed at night when he was very young. Of somebody named Larry who had once baled him out of a street fight by making like Bob Feller with some good-sized rocks...

But what was bed?

What was street-fights?

What was Bob Feller?

"I...guess so."

The room exploded in blinding light that seared his eyes and lanced his brain.

"Are you sure?"

"Oh yes! Oh God, yes!"

The agony was over and once again the room was mercifully black.

"You hate the cities."

The cities.

The decaying houses and the rotting tenements. The stinking alleys and the littered parks and the filthy buildings.

And the lawns and the happy kids and the beaches...

He didn't answer.

Somewhere within his mind a wheel started to spin. Slow. Then faster and faster until he was sweating and shaking with nausea and then it felt like he was flying apart into small fragments that tore and buffeted each other and pained...

Of course he hated the cities.

For a moment, peace.

"The apes. You hate the apes. You hate the human race."

The human race. *His* race. The pieces that were Stanley Martin started to flow together, to coalesce once more into a single individual...

And then his nerve endings and ganglions felt sharp, searing pain. Pain that threaded along his nerves and burned into every segment of his body, pain that threatened to fry his cortical centers.

Pain that scattered the particles of personality that were Stanley Martin and shriveled them to nothingness. Pain that obliterated the last traces of conscience and memory.

"You hate the human race," a voice repeated smoothly.

"Yes," Stan said, not hesitating. "I hate the human race." And then he started to sweat and shake with an unreasoning anger that flooded him as suddenly as if somebody had turned on a hose. The pain... The pain for which the apes were responsible.

"I hate the apes! I hate their damned guts!"

A silent wave of exultation swept the compartment. They had fashioned the mold and had made their monster...

Five minutes later, the space ship departed for its home system.

"I hate the human race."

CHAPTER FIVE

HE was 24 years old. A tall, unsmiling, handsome man dressed in a blue serge suit and a hat that he liked to pull down over his eyes so he could look at the world as if it were in a frame. He wasn't the type who made friends and there was a subtle air of menace about him that frightened the people with whom he came in contact. He was a stranger who looked at the world with cold and calculating eyes, like a scientist might look at a piece of lab apparatus. Women were intrigued by him, made their approaches, and hastily left—a little insulted and far more frightened.

Apes.

He was no longer 17, he was no longer a boy, and he wouldn't have shed a tear if he had been stretched on the rack. A hardness and a sense of power showed in the lines of his face and the set of his shoulders. People who talked to him felt inferior, as if they had been talking to a superman. And to a large degree they were absolutely right.

A small Thuscan flyer set him down one night on a fog-bound, Scotch moor, not far from Paisley. The next afternoon he had rented an apartment in Bristol and installed the first load of equipment. For the next three months, he did nothing but observe and travel—and buy up some small parcels of property in fifty different cities spread far and wide over the globe.

He started to set up an organization, though he had difficulty finding men to staff it. Most of those who would have qualified had been executed or were behind bars for life. But by the end of six months, his organization was almost complete. Reynolds, Langerman, and Caldwell were his lieutenants—the men who got their hands dirty and directed those in the next echelon down.

His right hand man was sent to him by Thusca. A powerful, urbane-looking man who smiled often with his mouth but never with his eyes. A guard let him in and he stood quietly in the rear of the room while Stan continued with his briefing session.

There were a dozen new men at the meeting, listening intently to what he had to say.

They were the type whose loyalty was to money, Stan thought, amused. Hard-faced men who had probably fought for a dozen different causes and switched sides as easily as changing a shirt.

Stan had almost finished with the briefing.

"Essentially, it's a simple smuggling operation. Only you're not to know what you're smuggling and under no condition are you to open your packages."

A man up front suddenly interrupted. "Why not?"

Stan smiled bleakly. "The packages are triggered, Piazza. I'm very much afraid if you tried to open it your head would be blown off. Satisfied?"

He turned back to the others.

"We pay very well—very well, indeed. A smart man, who isn't too curious, will find it well worth his while. We'll give you the packages and tell you where to leave them. In some cases, it will involve extensive travel on your part. Be cautious, be careful, and be quick on the trigger in case anybody tries to take them away from you."

THE man whom Stan had called Piazza stood up and started for the door. Stan watched him quietly until his hand was on the knob.

"What's the matter, Piazza?"

The man turned and spat on the carpet. "I don't like your proposition. I think it stinks. We take all the risks and we don't even know what we're doing!"

Stan shook his head sadly. "I'm sorry, Piazza. Really sorry. I had hoped we could use you."

Piazza whitened. "I'm no stoolie, Mr. Martin."

"We can't take the risk," Stan said simply.

In a movement that only one pair of eyes could follow, he reached inside his coat and shot through the cloth of the lapel.

Piazza looked faintly surprised and slumped limply to the floor.

Stan smiled coldly at the others. "I assume the rest of you can be counted on?"

After the others had left, the man in back walked up and introduced himself, flashing the small, fluorescent identity card that labeled him as having come from Thusca.

"Tanner." Stan frowned. "Funny, I think I've heard the name before but I can't place it."

"I met you briefly on Thusca," Tanner said easily.

Stan shook his head. "No, it's before then." He paused. "But that's impossible..."

Tanner raised his eyebrows. "Why?"

Stan looked surprised. "Didn't they tell you? Just before I started on this mission, I lost my memory. Crack on the head or something. I only saw two people before I left and they were busy filling me on what I was supposed to do here. Didn't have time to see the doctors." He walked to the liquor cabinet and started mixing himself a drink. "I'll be seeing Mr. Ainsworth and Mr. Malcolm in a few months and maybe they can help me then."

"You don't think your memory is liable to come back...here, do you?" Tanner asked curiously.

Stan laughed. "Not a chance—there's nothing that's apt to be familiar on *this* planet!" He dropped in the ice cubes. "Still, it's awkward. For all I remember of my past life. I might as well have been born in a vat."

Tanner smiled faintly. "I didn't know you were in the smuggling business."

"It's a good front and one in which we won't get our own fingers dirty. Besides, you haven't asked me what we were smuggling."

Tanner swirled his drink so the ice cubes clinked against the side.

"Alright, what are we smuggling?"

"Sometimes packages, sometimes suitcases, sometimes hat boxes. Our men take receipt of the packages and deliver them to different destinations where they think they're going to be picked up. Perhaps a broom closet in a building, perhaps a trash box on a city street, maybe a locker in a train station. There's only two things I haven't told the men— what's in the boxes, and the fact that they're never going to be picked up."

"What happens then?"

Stan sat down in a leather-upholstered chair and threw a leg over the arm. "Nothing. Not until November 4th, that is. At twelve noon, London time, half the cities of this world will be blown off the globe."

Tanner looked puzzled. "So? The air forces the fleets, and the armies will still be intact."

"They'll be much too busy to fight us," Stan said smoothly. "You see, Tanner, they'll be fighting each other."

Which actually was very clever, Stan thought slowly. The divide and conquer theory. Each of the packages contained a Thuscan fusion weapon. Once they were set off, each country would think that another had sprung a sneak attack.

November 4th, Tanner and he would strike. November 5th, the world would be in chaos.

November 6th, the Thuscan fleet would land.

Tanner walked to the middle of the room and stood over the body of Piazza. "What are you going to do with our friend?"

"Send him away—I think to Africa." Stan picked the body up and lugged it into what had once been the bedroom. Now it was a room jammed with transmitting equipment and, against the far wall, a single hoop of shining metal standing upright on a black marble base. The hoop was large, over six feet in diameter, with a thin, metal filament winding around it.

HE turned a dial set in the base.

The filament glowed red and then a brilliant white. The hoop itself shimmered and faded, while at the same time a whirling circle of brilliant black built up where it had been. He tensed his muscles and heaved and Piazza's body hit the circle and disappeared, like a man plunging into quicksand.

"Where will he land?"

"In a doorway on the Street of Lepers in Casablanca." Stan turned the dial again and the whirling circle slowed and became translucent and then faded out altogether as the hoop sprang back into view.

Tanner gestured to the other equipment. "What's all this for?"

"Transmitting equipment to set off the fusion packages." Stan pointed to two box-like structures against the far wall. One held a bank of fifty small, white lights. The other, a bank of fifty red. "The white lights are the operators themselves—I can tell immediately if anything happens to them. The others represent the fusion packages. If one of them goes, I know the package has been tampered with."

Even as he watched, one of the white lights flickered and died.

Tanner looked surprised. "What happened?"

"We just lost an agent," Stan said grimly. "Chicago sector." He glanced over at the bank of red lights—they were still lit. "It couldn't have been about the fusion packages. It must have been about the…other operation." He looked at Tanner. "The one you were sent to handle."

"What are you going to do about it?"

Stan shrugged. "We'll handle it ourselves, and then recruit another agent." He leafed through a filing cabinet, then finally pulled a dossier and gave it to Tanner. "Trace this man and find out what you can. We'll meet there in a week."

Tanner tapped the card lightly against his knuckles. "Mr. Ainsworth didn't think you'd be meeting any opposition."

Stan blanked his face of expression. He wasn't exactly sure why, but he didn't like Tanner.

"I didn't expect to."

There was a short silence and then Tanner walked to the hoop and worked the dial. The shimmering black sprang up and he stepped up on the marble. Just before he went through, he said: "What are you going to do about the...opposition?"

"When we find them, we'll smash them," Stan said coldly.

After Tanner had gone through, Stan shut off the hoop. As the circle faded it caught his image and held it briefly, like a mirror.

He stared at it abstractly.

The problem of possible opposition bothered him but there was something that worried him even more. Something he caught himself thinking about when he woke up in the morning. Something he thought about all day and something he couldn't get out of his mind when he went to bed at night.

Who was he?

CHAPTER SIX

IT was a summer evening and downtown Chicago was a hotbed of sweltering buildings and steaming tar streets. People stretched out on the lawns in front of Buckingham fountain for any stray breezes that might wander in off the lake or else they curled up in front of fans and read until the small hours of the morning when the temperature had drifted down a few degrees so it was possible to go to bed without drowning in a pool of their own sweat.

A woman walking by the Pure Oil building suddenly saw a shimmering in the air and then a man was standing in the shadowed doorway, staring nonchalantly at her. She almost screamed, then put it down to the heat and hurried by.

Stan strolled up Michigan Boulevard to stop for a moment in front of a bookstore where a man had been staring in the window.

"All set, Fred?"

Tanner nodded. "He leaves the Prudential building in half an hour. He parks his car on the ramp below the street, in the parking lot that runs parallel to the river. It's in the far corner—a sport model." He fumbled in his pocket for a small card. "Here's the license number. The ape is easy enough to recognize. About sixty years old, sport coat, and a pork-pie hat. He's had a small office here for a couple of weeks, doing government work, so he might be carrying a briefcase. Tomorrow he goes back east."

Stan memorized the description. "Just how good is he?"

"The best they've got. Losing him will be quite a blow to the apes. Quite a blow."

Stan stood in the shadows of the bookstore for a few minutes more. He could hear every tiny noise on the street, including the rapid tick-tick-tick of his own wristwatch.

"I better go down. Be ready to help with the body five minutes after the hour."

He turned and started up the street, to the stairs that would take him to the level below. Hundreds of cars were parked in neat, silent rows below the ramp. Overhead was the cold brilliance of hundreds of fluorescent lamps.

Light enough he thought. It wouldn't be...sporting...to shoot the ape scientist down in the dark.

He found the bright, two-toned sports car at the end of the ramp. Nobody was in sight. He smiled to himself and walked on past the car and then stood quietly in the shadows of a concrete pillar. He had a while to wait and disquieting thoughts swam slowly to the surface of his mind.

This city of Chicago. He had been to many cities on the planet but this was the only one that somehow...bothered him. A city that seemed oddly, tantalizingly familiar. And there was a pressing urgency for him to see some people in it...

But as an agent of Thusca, he could afford no time for such neurotic thoughts. He would tell the doctors about it when he returned, but right now there was work.

He stood there without moving a muscle, thinking of nothing at all, as if Stanley Martin were only an illusion and didn't really exist. It was a quarter to six.

Ten minutes to six.

Six o'clock.

And footsteps thudding on the concrete stairs a block away.

The man in the pork-pie hat was coming to get his car.

STAN set the stud on his heat gun and waited.

An ape.

The man came closer and fumbled at the door of his automobile, trying to get the key into the lock.

Stan pressed the stud and the violet beam flashed out and splashed on the car door six inches from the man's hand. The paint flared into a smoking fire and a neat, thin line raced down the metal, cutting cleanly through the body and the upholstery and the steel frame.

He'd let him squirm for a second, Stan thought coldly, and then move the beam back and cut the ape in two.

Now!

He never touched the man. There was a spanging sound and the pillar Stan was leaning against suddenly showed concrete chips. He fell backwards and sprawled on the pavement, the violet beam from his heat gun crazily scorching the concrete overhead.

Somebody yelled to the man crouched by the car...

"Run! Run, you fool!"

The man in the pork pie hat dodged up the ramp. Stan tried to pick him off but the pillar showered concrete again and his aim was spoiled. Then the man was gone and Stan's mind turned to his own problems.

The opposition had finally put in an appearance...

"Come out now and you can come out alive. Fight, and we'll bring you out dead!"

A woman's voice, he thought coldly. Coming from a car about a hundred feet down...

He aimed his heater and exploded the gas tank, the flames whooshing out into the closed space.

"You didn't think we were actually there, did you?"

He fired again and then a steady shower of concrete chips that sprayed his elbow made him glance at the pillar, alarmed. It had been cut entirely away at the top and now it was being chewed away at the bottom, ready to topple over on him.

He set his heater for a fan-shaped ray to cover his movements and scrambled out from behind the pillar, desperately trying to dodge over to the line of cars.

Something spanged into his shoulder and spun him around. He fell heavily to the pavement, the pain briefly paralyzing his nerves. He waited a split second for the pain to lessen, then tried to scramble for his heater. The cement in front of him exploded into dust and chips that cut his face and almost blinded his eyes.

"Get up!"

SHE stepped out from behind another pillar. A tall, black-haired woman with wide cheekbones and cold, green eyes. Her face was hard and she carried her hand weapon with all the assurance of one who was thoroughly familiar with it. Two men came with her. They were capable looking men but not the grim, hard-eyed professionals that Stan was used to working with.

The woman walked over to Stan and slapped his face—hard—her nails digging bloody furrows in his skin.

"How does it feel to be a traitor? How does it feel to sell out your native planet for nothing at all?"

He didn't know what she was talking about and his face showed it.

"It was a clever scheme," she continued bitterly. "To win a planet, you first cut off its head—you eliminate the scientists!" She leveled her hand weapon at him. "But that's not all you've had in mind. What other schemes has the renegade Earthman thought of?"

The world slipped into a haze of red and his hand darted for the pocket where he kept his heat gun—to pause, uncertainly, when he remembered it lay on the concrete fifteen feet away.

"I'm no ape!"

She laughed. "They've made you into a Pavlovian dog that drools whenever they ring a bell—and you don't even realize what they've done to you. They pull the strings and their marionette jerks and dances and does their dirty work for them!"

Stan stared at her coldly. "What are you going to do?"

"Kill you. Now."

She raised the weapon and Stan knew she was perfectly capable of doing it. A moment more and the small pellets would burrow into his body, to explode deep in the flesh. He tensed himself for a final effort to escape, knowing it would be next to useless.

"You poor fool," she said slowly. "You'll be better off dead."

Her finger tightened on the trigger.

She never pulled it. There was a scream behind her and one of her men collapsed to the pavement, a thin swirl of smoke drifting up from his blasted chest. The girl's eyes narrowed, then she suddenly darted towards the river that lapped against the parking level. The remaining man dropped to his knees to cover her escape and the ramp was filled with the spanging sound of his own pistol.

The sound ceased abruptly in another burst of flames and smoke and then Tanner was racing down the ramp.

"Don't let her get away!"

Stan ran to the river's edge and Tanner cut the oily surface with lancing rays from his heater.

"She's gone," Stan said in a tired voice. "Save it." He watched the surface for a moment more, than turned back to Tanner. "Who was she? What's her name?"

Tanner shrugged. "I don't know who she is or what she's doing here, I can't tell you."

He wouldn't forget her, Stan thought slowly. That long, black hair and those green eyes. And she had moved like a cat, a sleek cat that was just as willing to kill for a cause as he was.

Tanner was studying his face. "Don't get any ideas about her—she's an ape."

Stan looked at him coldly. "The only idea I have is to kill her before she kills me."

He started walking towards another flight of stairs a block down. How long had it been since he had walked down the ramp? He wondered. There had been the noise and the oily smoke from the automobile. The ramp should have been swarming with curious apes by now. But for some reason it wasn't...

It had shaken him, he thought slowly. His briefing on Thusca had mentioned nothing about an opposition organization of the apes. And in particular, it had mentioned nothing about a...girl.

He would have to warn the agents in his own organization, he thought abstractly. And it would probably be best to use a code name. He asked Tanner for a suggestion.

"Use a girl's name," Tanner mused. "Say...Avis."

Stan looked at him sharply and had the odd feeling that was really the girl's name. And then he recalled Tanner racing down the ramp screaming, *"Don't let her get away!"* And he recalled the disappointed look on his face when she had.

Tanner, Stan decided suddenly, had lied about not knowing her.

"She'll probably be around again," Tanner mused out loud. "And soon."

The second agent disappeared in Paris, two weeks later.

CHAPTER SEVEN

IT was eight o'clock Thursday evening when Stan stepped out of a faintly glowing circle of black light in a small alley off the Rue Pigalle in Paris. He calmly lit a cigarette and walked down the street to a small cafe.

It was bigger on the inside than it looked from the street. A long, low-ceilinged room with a tiny platform and a small band, almost hidden by the cigarette smoke at the far end. Tanner and Reynolds, one of Stan's lieutenants, were seated at a small table along the side, earnestly talking to a frightened little man with an old-fashioned walrus moustache.

Stan squeezed in next to the little man and introduced himself. He ordered wine, then said: "You know the arrangements?"

The little man looked stubborn. "I'm not sure I like it."

"We're not asking much—and we'll pay well."

The little man made a show of licking his lips and nervously twisting his moustache.

"I don't get you, guv'nor. You want to give me a hundred thousand francs just to deliver a package to the souvenir stand at the top of the Eiffel Tower?"

"You're to give the girl a hundred francs," Stan cut in smoothly. "And ask her if she'll hold it for a Monsieur Lorenz."

The little man's eyelids drooped suggestively. "You're up to no good and a hundred thousand francs doesn't seem to me to cover it."

Stan mover in closer, threateningly. The little man thrust out his chin and glared at him.

"Just you watch your step, guv' nor! All I 'ave to do is 'oller 'elp and fifty people will be on your neck. And what's to keep me from talking about this anyways?"

"I could kill you right while you sit there," Stan said quietly. "I could do it and you wouldn't make a sound and nobody would know you were dead until ten minutes after we left."

The little man's eyes showed white and he nervously twisted a heavy golden ring on his finger. "You wouldn't dare, guv' nor. A bloke like you wouldn't dare!"

"You'll do exactly as we say," Stan interrupted coldly. "And if we wanted you to, you'd do it for exactly nothing." He smiled grimly. "Your real name is William Clark. You're in this country without a visa or a passport. You jumped ship from a British freighter during the war. Your wife died shortly after you signed up for your last voyage and there was some talk about it. But you disappeared and they never found you again or heard from you and the case was dropped."

He paused. "Do you want me to go on?"

THE little man's eyes were wide and beads of sweat were dripping off the ends of his moustache.

"Why now, you wouldn't turn in an old man, would you, guv'nor? I've been clean ever since I been over 'ere! I 'aven't done a thing…"

Stan stared at him coldly. "Will you or won't you? You know the woman who runs the stand. It shouldn't be difficult."

The little man pretended to think about it for a moment.

"Why now, it doesn't seem like much," he mumbled. "Just a suitcase and you say all you want me to do is leave it with the woman?"

He had him, Stan thought.

"Be careful how you handle the suitcase and under no circumstances drop it—you'd be damned sorry if you did."

The little man drained his glass of wine. "When do I get my quid?"

"When we deliver the suitcase. Tomorrow."

The little man shivered and stood up.

"All right, I'll do it." He sidled past Tanner and stopped at the edge of the table. "Your eyes, guv' nor," he said suddenly, looking at Stan. "I swear to the Almighty, they're 'angman's eyes!"

Hangman's eyes.

Somewhere, someplace, Stan mused, he had thought that about somebody else. About Fred Tanner.

But he couldn't remember where it had been, or when.

Tanner fumbled in his wallet and gave the heavy man sitting next to him, a bill. "Reynolds, order up some more wine and see if they have any sandwiches, will you?" After Reynolds had left, he turned to Stan. "How many will this make?"

Stan ticked them off on his fingers.

"One in Chicago's Palmolive building, one in the Woolworth building on Manhattan Island, one in a dressing room of the Old Howard in Boston. Glasgow, Tokyo, Moscow, London, Rome and forty-one others. And now Paris. They're all covered. Fifty ape cities—none of them long for this world."

Tanner nodded thoughtfully.

"Mr. Ainsworth will be very pleased. Very pleased indeed."

Reynolds was back with a wine bottle in a small wicker basket and a plate of tired looking sandwiches. Stan drank the wine and ate the sandwiches without actually tasting them at all.

The cities were dirty, filthy ghettoes of brick and stone and the people were only apes, he mused. But somehow…

WILLIAM Clark lived in a small, stuccoed rooming house in a suburb midway between Paris and Versailles. It looked old even for a rooming house in France, Stan thought. There was a mustiness and an age you could sense even from the outside. The ivy that climbed the walls was dead, the stucco was chipped in spats, and the curtains on the other side of the windows looked yellowed and limp.

He climbed the front steps and worked the heavy knocker, then stood back waiting for the concierge to show up.

She didn't.

He tried the knocker again and then the doorknob. There was a sudden snapping sound, the door creaked open, and he stepped in.

Dust—billows of it—rose from the hall rug. Dust that almost choked him before it settled once more on an ancient window seat and clung to the moldering drapes.

He turned to Tanner and felt a shock of surprise. Tanner was cradling his heat gun in his hands, ready for instant action. His face was grim.

"What kind of a man would you say Clark was, Martin?"

"Offhand, kind of a tidy little man and…"

"Not the type who would be living in an ancient rooming house?"

"That's right—he wasn't the type."

"Where did Clark say he lived?"

"Second floor—end of the hall."

"Let's go…"

Stan hesitated a moment. He was supposed to be in charge of the operation, yet Tanner was taking over. For a very good reason—Tanner knew something that he didn't. He followed Tanner up the stairs, his feet sending out little puffs of dust from the stair treads. Clark's room was closed and he knocked lightly on the door.

There was no answer.

He tried the knob.

Locked.

"Reynolds—break it down."

The big man hunched his shoulders and drove for the door. The panel burst like it had been made from paper and he stumbled to the center of the room before he could stop himself.

"That was a foolish thing to have him do, Martin."

"Why?"

"You didn't know what to expect—it could have been a trap."

Stan's voice chilled. "You've been acting like a cat on a hot griddle ever since we walked in. Just what were you expecting?"

Tanner didn't answer. He sauntered into the room. "Well, where's Clark?"

That was a good question, Stan thought. Just where was Clark? He glanced around the room. The average rooming house cell, the kind so many people on this planet seemed to live in. A bureau and an unmade bed, the blankets rumpled and twisted...

THERE was a linen runner on top of the bureau and on top of that was a glass, neatly wrapped in cellophane. He walked over and barely touched it, intent on moving the glass to get a better look at a photograph behind it.

The cellophane cracked and crumbled at his touch.

The photograph behind it wasn't important, Stan thought. A photo of a ship on which Clark had been a crewmember.

What was important was the cellophane that had crumbled at his touch and the dusty linen runner that hung in tattered shreds where it overlapped the top of the bureau.

As if the weight of the cloth had become too much for the strength of the linen thread.

Old.

Incredibly old.

Tanner was standing by the window, looking out. When he moved back, his arm touched the curtain. The curtain collapsed and powdered, sifting down to the dusty carpet.

Stan watched it with intense curiosity, then moved over to the bed. The bedclothes were rumpled but they weren't lying flat. They were bunched in spots—as if somebody might still be underneath them.

He held his heat gun in one hand and flicked the blankets aside with the other. Like the curtains, they ripped and powdered.

Beneath the blankets was a skeleton—a few tattered pieces of cloth lying inside the gaunt bones. "I see you've found Clark," Tanner said.

"Clark?"

Stan could feel the sweat pop out on his forehead. Nobody on Thusca had ever told him that a man could die and the flesh on his bones shrivel to dust all in one evening. He bent over the bed. The skeleton was that of a man, a very old man, whose bones had started to calcify at the joints. There was nothing about it to link it with William Clark.

The little man with the walrus moustache had been middle-aged. He hadn't been old; he certainly hadn't been senile to the point where his joints were hardening.

Then he saw the ring on one of the finger bones. He touched it gingerly and rubbed away the green verdigris. The same ring he had seen Clark toy with at the tavern.

But the age! The incredible age!

He turned to Tanner, questioning. The narrow-eyed, dapperly dressed man was standing at one side of the window, his heat gun cocked. He was staring steadily through the glass and didn't bother to turn around. His voice was hard.

"You want to know what it's all about, don't you, Martin? Well, come on over and take a look for yourself."

"What about me?" a frightened voice suddenly rattled. "When's somebody going to tell me what's going on?"

Reynolds—they had forgotten all about him, Stan thought. Now the big man was shaking with fear, fear of the unknown. Stan wrinkled his nose. The ape was sweating and you could smell him clear across the room.

Tanner laughed easily. "I'll give you a full explanation later on, Reynolds. But right now we're in trouble."

CHAPTER EIGHT

STAN ran to the other window and stared at the street below. It didn't seem any different than when he had come in a few minutes earlier. The wide boulevard of stucco houses, the shade trees and the lawns. And a few of the apes on the sidewalk, hurrying to work...

Only they weren't hurrying, he noticed after a moment. One man was halfway down the house steps across the street, a brief case under his arm. But he wasn't moving. He was frozen in mid-air, off balance, one foot halfway down to the next step. A housewife had stopped in mid-stride two doors down, her shopping bag swung forward at an awkward angle. At the corner, a small Renault car was poised in the middle of the street, caught in the process of turning.

Further down the block, two small boys in short pants and berets had been playing catch. One was crouched, his hand out. The other was standing, one foot in the air and one upraised arm behind his head. Stan narrowed his eyes and located the ball. It was about ten feet from the thrower, crawling slowly through the air.

Even as he watched, the ball slowed and stopped, hovering twenty feet above the asphalt.

"The air!" Reynolds suddenly screamed. "It's getting hard to breathe!"

"It'll get harder!" Tanner said grimly. "This will last for about half an hour. Slow your breathing and whatever you do, move slow. You move too fast and the air friction alone will set your clothes on fire!"

He swung slowly forward and brought the butt of his heat gun against the glass. Small cracks lanced through the window but it didn't break. Tanner pushed against it and the pieces slowly folded outwards.

"We're in the fast field, Martin—and so are they."

"They?"

"Avis and her men. The one who caught you flat-footed under the ramp the other day. They're the ones who put up the field who killed Clark."

Clark.

Avis, Stan thought, could probably speed things up as well as slow them down. Clark was to have stayed home today, to wait for them. Avis and her men had waited until everybody but Clark had left, then they had turned on the field and aged the house and Clark by a hundred years in five minutes. It explained the skeleton, it explained the dust, it explained the crumbling cellophane and the yellowed curtains that powdered at the touch.

And the day on the ramp in Chicago. Avis had speeded things up, then. What had seemed to him to take half an hour, had actually occurred in minutes.

"How come we're not standing still like the others?"

"Neutralizers—they're built into your belt. If they weren't, you could have died a long time ago. Our own fields shield Reynolds."

He broke off.

"Here they come!"

ACROSS the street a figure darted from one parked car to another. A man suddenly ran behind the car that was poised on the corner. Stan could make out other figures moving behind the windows across the street.

There was the familiar spanging sound and a series of holes stitched themselves in the fragments of glass left in the window frame, three inches from his cheek. There was an impression of speed and heat and a crackling sound as the tiny projectiles thudded into the plaster behind him.

A pale, violet glow flashed out from Tanner's window and one of the figures on the street suddenly raised its hands in agony as flames crisped its clothing and burned its flesh. It staggered a few feet and finally fell in a flaming mass, its screams of agony splitting the still air.

Stan let his breath out slowly. He hadn't got a good look at the figure and for one brief moment he had thought it was…Avis.

Which was an odd way to feel about a woman who would gladly slit his throat, he thought.

"One!" Tanner said grimly.

Stan flamed one of the automobiles and narrowly missed a small figure that scuttled out from behind it. He stole a look at Tanner. The man's face was flushed and shining, a half grin of expectancy was painted on it.

He did it as a duty, Stan thought of himself soberly.

But Tanner enjoyed killing.

The spanging sounds sounded harder. Outside the window frames, Stan could see gouts of concrete and stucco being chiseled out of the walls. There was practically nothing left of the frames themselves but splinters of wood, held in place by small lumps of disintegrating mortar.

They were taking the house apart, he thought. They were dissecting it as casually as you would a frog, until the entire front part of the room would be exposed and there would then be no place to hide.

He turned up a notch on his heater and sprayed the other side of the street with a wide-angle beam. There was an abrupt cessation of noise and then it started in again, louder than before. The small bedroom was becoming foggy with concrete and brick dust.

He caught sight of a figure moving behind the shrubs across the street and took careful aim. There was a sharp cry and then he had to dodge quickly back inside the window. Something had grazed his cheek, cutting it so a thin stream of blood angled down from the cheekbone.

He waited a second and stole another quick look out.

Two men had taken refuge behind some trees, further down the block. He took aim, then hesitated. The frozen figures of the two boys who had been playing catch were directly in the line of fire.

He tightened his finger, then sweat crept into the corners of his eyes and he blinked for a moment. He took aim again...and wavered slightly. The sweat was heavier now and he could feel it soak the shirt on his back. Once more...only apes...

"What are you waiting for?"

Stan calmly chose another target.

"The apes that are hiding—they won't stay there forever. They'll move someplace else and when they do, I'll get them."

TANNER laughed and aimed out the window. A moment later, two blazing torches had crumpled to the asphalt. Almost simultaneously, the trees went up in flames and two fiery figures stumbled out from behind them.

"Don't ever let your emotions interfere with your better judgment," Tanner said shortly. "Mr. Ainsworth wouldn't like it. Neither would I."

Stan hardly heard him. It didn't mean anything to him one way or the other, he kept telling himself. They were apes. Just apes.

"What will the apes say when this is over and they discover the shattered houses and the bodies?"

Tanner picked off another running figure.

"There'll be no bodies. The wind disperses the ashes as soon as the field is let up. As for the rest—the apes are ingenious in thinking up explanations. They never believe in anything they haven't seen themselves."

The room was thick with dust and the noise of the spanging; the front wall was holed in half a dozen different spots. Then there was a rush of figures across the street and Stan caught his breath. In the lead was Avis, black hair streaming, urging the others on...

Tanner suddenly ran to the back of the room and pushed the bureau and the bed over by the front wall. He stripped the closet and piled the clothes by the furniture.

There was a lull in the spanging and a quiet sobbing suddenly filled the room. Stan turned.

Reynolds had collapsed in a corner, half out of his mind with fear. Tears straggled down the big man's face and sobbing convulsed his chest.

Tanner gestured to the front wall. "Get over there, Reynolds!"

The frightened man half-crawled, half-stumbled over to the tumbled furniture.

"You wanted an explanation, didn't you?" Tanner asked sharply.

Stan knew what was coming. Reynolds had ended up by knowing too much. Which was just too bad for Reynolds.

Reynolds' frightened babbling gradually made sense.

"Get me out of here, Mr. Tanner! Please get me out of here..."

"Gladly," Tanner said grimly.

He brought up the heater and a violet beam danced over the crouching man and the bureau and the piled clothing. There was a short, pitiful screaming and then flames shot high into the room and billows of smoke curled casually through the broken windows.

SOMETHING inside Stan felt sick and he cursed himself for his own weakness.

"Get the suitcase and let's go, Martin."

The suitcase.

It wasn't there. While they had been busy at the windows, Stan thought, somebody had stolen the case. Reynolds hadn't even seen them and even if he had—the ape was now beyond questioning.

"It's gone?" Tanner laughed. "Avis is an amateur, Martin. And a bungling amateur at that! She could have killed us again and instead she preferred the case! One call to Ainsworth and we'll replace that tomorrow!"

They were feeling their way down the back stairs when the thick feeling to the air disappeared. Suddenly the street was filled with screams as passersby's noticed the instantaneously ruined house and the burning cars and the suspicious mounds of ashes that swirled up into the morning air.

A block away, Stan stopped and wiped the sweat and soot from his face. Tanner looked at him sharply. "Something wrong?"

"Yes, there's something wrong!" Stan swung around and grabbed Tanner by the lapels, crossing his hands so the cloth was drawn tight around Tanner's throat and his knuckles dug into the flesh.

"I haven't been getting the answers," he said in a thin voice. "The girl's no ape—she knows too much, her weapons are too far advanced, her men are too well organized!" His voice started to shake with nervous reaction. "I'm supposed to be running the operation down here and I don't even know what's going on!"

"The answers should have occurred to you," Tanner said, his face a mask. "We're not the only ones who want this planet, Martin!"

Not the only ones! Stan relaxed his grip and let his arms hang limply at his side.

"Avis is an Aurellian," Tanner went on. "Her system and ours have fought many bloody battles for this planet. We're still fighting them—down here, now." He paused. "You haven't been told everything—operators are fed knowledge bit by bit, when they can fit it in. As a Thuscan agent, Martin, you're told just as much as the high command thinks necessary!"

His voice softened, became more persuasive. "We kill but not blindly, Stan. This is an important war—it's a war for an entire planet. We have to be brutal but the stakes are high. We're fighting to capture this planet for our own...flesh and blood."

"I'm sorry," Stan whispered. "Forget what I did."

He wouldn't make the same mistake again, he thought. He'd do what he was told and he wouldn't forget that Avis and all of her kind were his implacable enemies, the enemies of his people.

But there was still something that bothered him.

In talking to him, Tanner had sounded like somebody he had heard once before...

CHAPTER NINE

THE nightmares started in Beirut. Stan's apartment was a modern one, just a block from the American University. He had opened the wood-slat Venetian blinds and had gone to bed, feeling dead tired. It was late August and things had not gone too well. Agents had disappeared. Fusion packages had disappeared from their hiding places.

But worries could not compete with physical exhaustion. He was asleep as soon as he hit the pillow.

The nightmares were terrifying. He was no longer Stanley Martin, patriotic agent for the planet Thusca. He was 17 years old once more, playing in the city streets of Chicago and fighting in a pillow fight with his older brother and running errands for his mother or watching her while she made meat loaf and took loaves of freshly baked bread from the ovens.

And then there was the smell of printing ink on freshly printed papers and reporters yelling "Copy boy!" at him and the twice-weekly trips to the stockyards to pick up the live stock reports.

The stockyards. He had stopped by an alley one morning and three men had jumped him, slugging him in the stomach and kidneys and hitting…hitting…hitting…

He woke up, shaking. His pajamas and the bed sheets were soaked with perspiration. He sat on the edge of the bed and held his head in his hands.

He had dreamt that he was an ape.

He got up and went to the bathroom for a glass of water. He didn't go back to sleep.

The nightmare the next night was different. Once again he saw two small French boys playing in the street. One moment, thin, bandy-legged kids in short pants and berets…the next, two blazing torches that crumpled silently to the asphalt.

And then there was the hideous, horribly shrill screaming of Reynolds when Tanner had played the heat gun over him. The terrible screaming that Stan knew would haunt him for years…

He woke up again, rolled to the side of the bed, and was sick.

The nightmares, the damned nightmares… He fumbled for matches and cigarettes on the bed table. The tiny flame of the match shook nervously in the gloom of the bedroom.

He *had* to stop the nightmares, even if it meant dosing himself with drugs before he went to bed. He couldn't stand the dreams; he couldn't take the false memories that kept cropping up.

The next night he made up his mind. There were pieces still missing from the puzzle of who he was. There were things, he felt sure, that Tanner had never told him. Things, no doubt, that the high command had felt he wasn't ready to know yet.

A good agent wouldn't question higher authority, he thought slowly, sweating. But he *had* to know! He had to know the answers; he had to know about his first 25 years of life.

And there was one person who might be able to give him some information. One person who had once called him a traitor, who had implied he was a renegade and had been conditioned. One person who knew things about himself that he didn't.

The girl, Avis.

Eventually, he had to find her—to kill her. But right now, he wanted to find her to get information.

HE got dressed, set the dial of the transport-hoop for London and stepped through. Tanner was waiting for him on the other side.

"Where is she?" Stan asked.

Tanner raised his eyebrows.

"The North American continent. Chicago."

"Exactly where?"

"I don't know…exactly. We've been trying to trace the radiations from the fusion package but it keeps moving about the city." Tanner grimaced. "We haven't been successful in following it. We've lost quite a number of agents trying to follow it, as you know."

He stood up and fished in his pocket for a pipe and a small pouch of tobacco. He looked very casual, very urbane, Stan thought.

"You going after her, Martin?"

"That's right—I'm going after her."

Tanner studied him curiously.

"You're taking a risk. Our agents will locate her sooner or later."

"They haven't so far," Stan said sarcastically. "Why leave it to chance?"

Tanner shrugged. "Good luck." Then he added seriously: "Don't talk to her, Martin. Don't give her a chance to pull something. Kill her on sight."

"I'll do that," Stan lied. He checked his heat gun, then worked the dial on the hoop once more and stepped through the shining oval...

...onto a street on Chicago's south side, a few doors down from the Hyde Park theatre. He walked into a nearby drug store and made a phone call, then walked back to the corner to wait. A moment later, one of his chief lieutenants, Caldwell, drove up.

"We lost Jones and Hagerty, Mr. Martin—just a few hours ago. I was making up a report on them when you called."

"You got the indicator?"

The man held out a small gadget that looked a little like a light meter. Stan swung it around experimentally. A small light mounted on it flickered briefly. He swung it back again and the light glowed, went out, and then glowed strongly again.

"You know, I don't see how you trace a person with that," Caldwell said, curious. "How does it work?"

There were a lot of things that Caldwell didn't know, Stan thought. He didn't know that the deal was anything more than a smuggling operation, he didn't realize that this was not a gang war but was one for much higher stakes but if his curiosity kept up, some day he would stumble on the truth.

Which would be rather fatal for Mr. Caldwell.

"You're paid for what you do, Caldwell, not for being curious."

"Okay, okay—I just asked."

Stan slid into the back seat. "Let's go."

Caldwell threw the car in gear and they drove silently north through the crowded streets. The light on the small indicator waxed and waned and grew steadily brighter as the faint radiation from the fusion material increased.

"You don't want to get too close," Caldwell said suddenly. "That's what happened to the other boys. They got too close and then they were ambushed."

The indicator light slowly increased in brilliance, then started to die again. They were about three blocks away, Stan thought, passing it at right angles.

"Okay, Caldwell, let me out here."

"You sure you won't need help, Mr. Martin? I could get some of the boys..."

"Wait on the corner. If I'm not back in an hour, then notify Tanner. He'll know what to do."

He got out of the car, palming the indicator in his hand. Avis—or at least the package—was somewhere in the area.

He glanced at the indicator and started walking, stopping occasionally to look in a store window and steal another look at the indicator. A block and a half down. One door, two door...

And back one.

An office building. The usual miscellany—dentists and doctors and small professional firms.

He walked in, his eyes documenting everybody in the lobby. Any two or three of the men idling in the lobby could be her men, he thought.

And if anyone of them had made a false movement, there would have been a sudden massacre.

"Top floor, please."

The elevator crept slowly up and let him out on the fifth floor.

The reaction on the indicator was strong. He went down to the fourth floor where it was stronger, then down to the third.

The second floor and the light dimmed slightly. It was the third floor then.

He walked quietly back up the stairs and paused at the landing, listening. There were no sounds of anyone in the corridor. He walked casually down it. A doctor's office, a dentist's office, a hairdresser's, and an employment agency.

The employment agency, he thought sharply. The perfect front, the perfect cover.

The perfect way to recruit agents.

He stopped quietly outside and unlimbered his heat gun from its shoulder holster. He turned the knob and walked in.

And was suddenly aware that all noise had stopped, the air was heavy, and the dust motes in the stream of sunlight that lanced through the window were perfectly still.

"YOU took a long time getting here, Martin."

She was standing in front of her desk, looking exactly as when he had seen her on the ramp in Chicago and on the street in the Paris suburb. A tall woman, a little on the thin side. Thick black hair that hung loosely about her face, making a frame for a pale skin and cold, green eyes. It was a hard, capable face with just a suggestion that at another time and another place, it might have been a beautiful face.

Now... A drawn face, with a tinge of sadness to it.

Stan leveled his heat gun. She didn't move a muscle but patiently waited for him to press the stud.

Don't talk to her, Tanner had said. Kill her on sight. But he hadn't come to kill her. Not yet. Not before he found out some information.

He lowered his arm.

"Don't tell me you've finally gotten sick of killing people," she said quietly.

"No doubt it runs into hundreds," Stan said sarcastically. "I suppose any day now the apes will be getting suspicious."

She shook her head, bitterly. "No—they won't. It happens all the time. People die in lonely little rooms, people have accidents, people commit suicide. Or so the Terrans think. They never seem to look beyond."

"You forget," Stan pointed out. "We've lost men, too. And I'm sure that not all of them died from natural causes."

"Who have you lost, Martin? Thieves, dope peddlers, murderers, and worse? And what have I lost? Patriots, scientists, statesmen—the few who understand and believe and are willing to work with me."

Stan shrugged impatiently. "You said I had taken a long time in getting here. I suppose you planned it that way."

She looked surprised. "Why else do you think we stole the fusion packages? Just to keep you from replacing them? The Thuscans can supply you with all the packages you need. We wanted to give you something by which you could trace me."

"It's a wonder you weren't killed before this."

A half smile broke the granite lines of her face. "Nobody but you would have gotten this far, Martin."

"So you got me here. What do you want?"

She looked at him thoughtfully for a full minute, weighing him.

"I want you to change sides, Martin. I want you to help us."

He stared at her in disbelief. "You must have known I wouldn't agree—even before you asked me."

"We need your help," she said steadily.

"You're doing all right."

"We're losing," she said, her face looking even more pale. "We've lost close to three hundred agents and we've located only ten fusion packages. I don't know your exact timetable but I know it's sometime in November. It's late August now." Her face twisted. "We haven't got a chance, and you know it…"

"That's right," he agreed. "You haven't got a chance. What do you want me to do? Sell out?"

"You've already sold once," she said brutally.

There was that hint again, he thought sharply. The hint that she knew something about himself that he didn't. Or at least, she thought she did.

"Why should I sell out to a group of aliens?" he asked curiously.

"Because we're not a group of aliens," she said calmly. "Because this planet is *our* planet, everybody on it is an Aurellian. And so are you..."

"You expect me to believe that?"

"It's true!" she blazed. "But you've been conditioned. You believe everything the Thuscans tell you and you've never questioned it. Now it's time somebody told you the truth!"

SHE leaned closer to him and he caught a trace of faint perfume. "This whole world could go up in smoke, Martin, and it actually wouldn't be important. Not to the Thuscans and not to my own people. You know why? Because it's a sidelight. An unimportant little skirmish in a battle your mind couldn't even conceive of."

"You're lying," he said, without conviction.

She walked to the window and gestured outside.

"This Earth—it's not the home of the human race, Martin. It's a colony planet—colonized thousands of years ago, like a hundred other systems. For the last fifty thousand years, Aurelia has expanded throughout the galaxy. We don't keep contact with all the planets we've colonized—we can't. Our mission was to sow the human race far and wide and let them develop as they would.

"That was a mistake." She walked back to the desk. "Eventually we ran into the Thuscans—your so-beloved friends, Martin. They were expanding too, toward us. We had to fall back to try and defend our primitive little colony planets. And that wasn't easy. It wasn't easy at all."

Her face clouded and the look of sadness deepened.

"We had been peaceful for too long. And we weren't professional militarists. And we were so few. So pitifully few! The most we could hope to do was to combat the Thuscan system of infiltration, and then try to convince each planet of its own peril, so they could look to their own defenses."

Stan sneered. "You haven't been successful, have you?"

"What do you think would happen if we showed ourselves and set down a ship?" she asked curtly. "Most of the planets would be paralyzed with terror. They'd consider us suspect and they would hate us because we were more advanced. I do what I can. I try to convince a few. And when I do, they usually try to help." She looked at him again and her face was sheer hate. "Patriotic men, Martin—men that you've helped to slaughter!"

For a fraction of a second, she looked like she was going to break down. Then her face hardened again. Her voice was husky.

"I've manned the barricades on a thousand different planets, Martin. I've fought the Thuscans for as long as I can remember. Sometimes I've succeeded, more often I've failed. And when I've failed, I've had to run away." Her voice changed to steel. "But I'm not running anymore. If I lose, I'm staying here."

"You picked the wrong person to give a speech to," Stan said coldly. He started for the door and then stopped. "You said I was an Aurellian, a human being. What did you mean by that?"

"You were born in this city 25 years ago," she said in a low voice. "You worked here, your family lived here. You had a mother and a brother named Larry. You were…exceptional. All the indications are that you would have made a great man. You loved the world and the people in it. When you were seventeen, you were kidnapped by the Thuscans and conditioned to be what you are now. They intentionally made you lose your memory, so that you would have no memories and no will—no will but theirs."

"I don't believe you," he said heavily.

"You don't want to." She paused. "You better leave, Martin. You better go back to the marionette makers and the string pullers."

He took one last look, realizing that something inside him was struggling to give the girl comfort, to say something that might help her. Then he shrugged and walked out the door.

He was two blocks away before he realized that both he and the girl could have killed each other at almost any time.

But neither of them had made any attempt to.

CHAPTER TEN

HE was two men, after the meeting with the girl, Stanley Martin, the loyal Thuscan agent who continued to mastermind the betrayal of a world.

And Stanley Martin, the man who wondered at and was repelled by his own action. The man to whom the city of Chicago was strangely familiar. The man who distrusted Tanner and who knew there was a reason for it. The man in whose mind small bits of memory kept bobbing to the surface, like a ship that was breaking up beneath the sea and planks and spars kept rising to the top.

He also knew that that way lay…madness. Two minds could not continue to dwell in the same body. He could not continually war with himself. The weaker, the fainter of the two would have to die.

Which meant that the person who had brought his weaker memory to the surface would have to die.

Avis was slated for death.

He worked at it consciously and carefully. One of the fusion packages was planted in a small store in Chicago, near the intersection of 63rd and Halsted. One of Avis' agents tried to pick it up and was killed. Two more tried the next day—and failed.

The word filtered out that the package was a special package, that its importance overshadowed that of other fusion packages. But no more agents tried for it.

By the end of October, opposition had apparently dwindled and faded. Avis had vanished from sight. There were reports that she had been seen in Stockholm and once that she had been glimpsed in a Moscow suburb. Then the reports ceased entirely.

Stan was not deceived. Avis would try once more, he thought. She would try for the package in Chicago. So he prepared for her, for the final ambush.

The 31st of October, agents were reported filtering down to the intersection and Stan decided to step in personally.

He stepped out of the circle of shimmering light in an alley near 63rd street. Nobody noticed him at all. People were streaming past him, racing through the alley to get away from the intersection. Stan grabbed a man running past him.

"What's going on?"

The man was sweating with fear, his eyes rolling wildly.

"Damn, mister, don't go out there! They got guns that shoot flames and there's fifty people lying dead in the intersection! All in a minute. I'm walking past on my way to Sears and all of a sudden the streets are loaded with corpses!"

Stan let him go and raced up the alleyway. He could hear the quiet, singing noises of the heat guns and the rapid, spanging gunfire of Avis' men. She had come out in the open, trying desperately to convince the apes that they were threatened by alien groups. She had turned off the time projector halfway through the battle and it must have seemed like carnage had sprung up instantaneously.

There were at least two dozen crumpled figures lying on the pavement near the intersection. Some were crisped to near ash and others had been blasted with the spanging pellets. Two cars were blazing furiously and the windows in Sears and Wieboldt's had been shattered.

A pellet whizzed past his ear and he ducked low, glancing swiftly around the intersection. A thin, violet beam was playing from a doorway in Sears and he dodged toward it, ignoring the other spanging projectiles that ripped through the air and caromed off the building walls behind him.

Tanner was in the doorway, nursing a bleeding shoulder, his face glowing with the joys of battle.

"Tanner, what happened?"

"She's playing it in the open," Tanner snarled. "She's trying to convince the apes that way!"

She might succeed, Stan thought slowly, but it was more likely that the apes would blame it on a gang war of some kind. They wouldn't believe the truth. They wouldn't want to.

Tanner pointed down the street a block. "Cover it down there and we'll try to drive them toward you!"

Stan raced down half a dozen doors, then suddenly stiffened. There was the wail of sirens. And then the heavy chatter of a machine gun and the drifting choking of tear gas.

The spanging sounds and the violet beams suddenly stilled and figures slipped quietly from the buildings toward the side streets. Stan hesitated and then started running, away from the intersection.

He collided with Avis when she darted from a doorway. The granite face had broken and tears were streaking down it. Before he realized it, he was holding her tightly around the shoulders while she sobbed into his chest.

He had been fooling himself all along, he suddenly knew. He couldn't kill her. He couldn't come anywhere near to it.

He didn't want to.

"In every game," he said quietly, "there has to be a side that wins and a side that loses."

Her sobs broke off and she looked up at him, shaking her head to clear the hair from her face.

"I'm not crying because I've lost," she said quietly. "I'm crying because...a brave man is dying! Because so many brave men have died!" She paused and the lines of weariness etched themselves back into her face. "I should have told you, Stan. I should have told you long ago. Maybe it might have helped."

She pointed to the intersection.

"He won't...last long. Go out and say goodbye."

HE stared back at the intersection. It was quiet now, powdered concrete dust settling slowly out of the air. Police were circling among the quiet forms lying on the pavement while curious onlookers began to form a ring around the corner.

He walked quietly back to the street.

"Over here, Stan." The voice was faint. "You better...hurry!"

A figure was slumped by one of the cars, its whole left side a singed and blackened mass of ash.

Stan walked over to him. The man coughed and spewed a gout of red over the front of him. "We always wondered what had happened, Stan...Mom and me. And then Avis found me and told me you had sold out." The low hacking cough again and a spasmodic heaving of the chest. "N—never believed it. You weren't the type." His eyes closed in brief pain. "Told her that a hundred…a thousand times, I guess." He paused for a moment and Stan thought he was gone. Then the eyes flickered open.

"I was g—gonna break the whole story in tomorrow's editions. Guess…your man got wind of it."

Stan couldn't bring himself to look down at the left side where the clothing was burned and where half of the waist was carbonized. He knew Tanner's work with the heater and he knew how well the man liked to see his victims squirm.

The cough started in again and suddenly the man was sitting up, his face twisted with pain and tears. *"Y—you don't even remember me! Y—you d—don't even remember your own damned brother!"*

And just before he died he said: "I'm s—sorry, Stan. God bless…"

And then he was gone and Stan knew that the man he was holding was nothing more than dead clay. He crouched there, his face wet, and the bits and tiny pieces of personality that had once been Stanley Martin coalesced and recombined into the individual they had been eight years before.

He stood up, the tears streaming down his face, and looked down at his brother Larry. A flood of memories were surging back. The games they had played, the arguments they had had, the way they had stuck up for each other…

And he could remember that morning when he had been slugged and the Thuscans had picked him up. Mr. Malcolm and Mr. Ainsworth and Tanner and the knives and the machines that had broken his spirit.

Somebody tapped him on the shoulder. A policeman had his notebook out and was looking at him curiously.

"You knew this man?"

"Once," Stan said slowly. "A long, long time ago."

He turned and walked up the street.

"Hey, you can't go! We need your help for questioning!"

He had more important business, Stan thought. With Mr. Ainsworth and Mr. Malcolm.

And his fellow renegade, Tanner.

AVIS was waiting for him in the alley, standing in the shadows by the circle of whirling black. Her face wasn't the collection of hard planes and angles it usually was and he realized dimly there was a beauty about her he had never appreciated before. A beauty and a certain sympathy...

He stood helplessly and looked at her. There was nothing he could say.

There was nothing *to* say. He had betrayed his world and she knew it.

"It's not too late," she said quietly.

He shook his head. "It's all over but the gloating." He felt himself start to shake. *"My God, I've condemned a world to death!"*

"You can stop it."

"There's no time!"

"There's four days."

Four days, he thought wildly.

Four days in which to recover fifty fusion packages hidden in cities that circled the globe. Four days in which he had to baffle his own agents...and Tanner.

"I'm only one man, Avis. I could try—but I wouldn't make it."

"If you want help," she said, "all you have to do is ask."

She still had her own organization, Stan thought. It wasn't as large as his own but its members were willing to die for a cause and they were brave and courageous. They didn't have the advantage of the transport-hoops, but then they were already spread out around the globe. It would be easy for Avis to communicate with them.

All he had to do was to give her the locations. And then, between himself and her agents…

It might be possible at that.

"All right, he said grimly. "Let's try it." He checked his heat gun and the two of them stepped through the shimmering haze…

…into the apartment in Bristol. He cautioned Avis to be quiet, and then opened the door silently into the living room. Tanner wasn't there but his lieutenant, Langerman, was. A small, wiry man with a rodent's face and sliding eyes who preferred looking at the small of a man's back rather than looking him straight in the eyes.

It had been necessary for Tanner and he to include one man in their confidence, one man who would hold down the fort in Bristol and watch the panels that marked the location of the fifty fusion packages and the agents.

Langerman was sitting by the fusion package panel, reading a newspaper.

He looked up when Stan stepped into the room. "How's it going, boss?"

"It's going all right," Stan said casually. He reached into his pocket for some money. "How about going down to the corner and having some lunch sent up? Anything that looks good."

LANGERMAN grabbed the coin, shrugged, and sauntered towards the door. "Sure thing. Sandwiches and tea."

As soon as he was gone, Stan motioned Avis into the room and started writing down the exact locations of the fusion packages. Suddenly there was a voice behind him.

"Hey, what's going on? How'd the chick get in?"

Langerman had come back, his shirt faintly spattered with raindrops. He had gotten as far as the front door, Stan thought, discovered the state of the weather, and come back for a raincoat.

Nothing was going right...

It was to late for explanations. Langerman's hand had snaked beneath his suit coat and come out with a small pistol.

"Tanner would like to hear about this," he said, his eyes narrow.

He should have thought of that long ago, Stan thought coldly. Tanner hadn't trusted him, never had. Tanner had watched him. And when Tanner wasn't around to do the watching, he had made sure that somebody else was.

He didn't argue. He straightened out and dove for Langerman's legs. There was a sharp report and a splintering sound behind him and then Langerman was down, frantically trying to hit Stan in the face with the pistol butt.

Stan rolled him violently against the wall and grabbed for the hand that held the pistol. He caught it and tried to force it back. The two arms wavered, then Langerman began to give a little, his arm moving slowly back.

A world was in the balance, Stan thought grimly, and with a surge of strength he had the pistol. He slashed at Langerman's head and the little man went limp.

He stood up and thrust the list into Avis' hand. "There it is—all fifty. I've marked the ones I'll try to work myself."

She took the list and started back to the whirling circle.

"We'll meet again?" he pleaded.

"Right here," she said calmly. "On November 4th."

He watched her disappear, then worked the dials for another destination and stepped through to the unknown.

He had four days, he thought, in which to save a world.

Four short days.

CHAPTER ELEVEN

THE night clouds rolled across the steeples of Bristol and the muffled voice of a church clock somberly rolled across the city, striking the hour of ten. The hush of a chill autumn night lay across the city, mantling the fog that started to deepen in the city streets.

In a small apartment on Regent Street, a box-like machine sat quietly in a corner, staring at the growing gloom with fifty red, unwinking eyes.

At five minutes after the hour, there was a flickering and then there were only forty-nine. By eleven o'clock, the eyes had been cut down to forty-six.

The evening of the first, there were only thirty-nine.

By the third, there was only a dozen. And every hour that went by saw another light wink out...

He stood in a Moscow subway station, watching the trains thunder past and keeping an eye on a trash can in a little niche near an elaborate mosaic of Malenkov. None of the comrades, he thought, would think of depositing litter near the mosaic of the leader and so the can had never been used.

And since the cleaners knew it was never used, there was no earthly reason why it should have to be disturbed and emptied. So the can sat there and had never been touched.

Except once.

For a moment the platform was deserted and Stan walked rapidly back to the can. A moment later he held the fusion package in his hand...

Somebody barked something at him and he looked up, startled.

A few yards away, there was a man in the uniform of the people's police. He could have been hiding for any one of a number of reasons, Stan thought. He could have been watching for petty thievery or perhaps there had been a drive against littering the platforms.

But it didn't matter why he was there. The point was he was asking questions in Russian and Stan couldn't answer him.

Another train roared in and people poured out of it, crowding together on the platform. Stan turned and darted for a washroom, breaking the wrappings on the fusion package as he ran. A moment later he had snapped the detonating wires and broken the delicate, clockwork mechanism and the almost infinitesimally small transceiver.

He threw the remains of the package under the wheels of the train at the same time a pistol shot roared above his head, chipping off some of the tile of the ceiling.

Then he had made it to the washroom door, passed his hand over a brass plaque, and darted through the circle of black that appeared into...

...a dark corner of a bazaar in Damascus.

The bazaar stretched down both sides of the street, terminating against a mosque at one end. There were small, open shops that sold copperware and incense burners and large metal dishes, ornately tooled. There were tables and boxes of elaborate mosaic worktables with veneers of rare wood and inlaid with mother of pearl. There were small restaurants and notion stores and shops that displayed bolt after bolt of silk and brocade.

STAN watched the people wandering past, then brushed past a small native boy begging for coins, and walked into one of the silk shops.

"Yes, M'sieur?"

"You're holding a bolt of brocade for a Mr. Liebman. May I see it please?" Stan flashed a card.

The little clerk waddled to the back of the store and returned with a small bolt of silk. Stan reached for it but the small man held it back.

"You are Mr. Liebman?"

Stan was sweating. "I'm a friend of his."

"I'm sorry, M'sieur. I was told not to release this to anybody but Mr. Liebman."

The little man wanted to stand and argue while the world went up in flames, Stan thought. He pulled out his wallet and slid a five dollar bill across the counter.

"I don't think Mr. Liebman would want this quite as much as I would."

The little man was not convinced. "Perhaps not but..."

Stan thrust out the flat of his left hand and pushed the clerk back against the shelves. Bolts of cloth rippled down from them and Stan had to dig beneath them to get the one he wanted.

A moment to open the bolt and cut the wires of the package and then he was out in the street once more, the clerk's shrill, indignant screams echoing after him.

He raced to the end of the street, near the mosque, for the dark corner that looked a little too dark and a little too glossy and then...

...out again in a small street a block from the Vatican in Rome. It was early evening. Twelve more hours to go, he thought, for the last one. That wouldn't take long and he could double check any that Avis' agents might have missed.

He hailed a taxi and sped out to the ruins of the old Forum. He waited until the taxi had left and then walked over to the column of Trajan—the tall, marble column that had been erected in order to commemorate the victories and the accomplishments of the old Roman emperor. He vaulted the low iron fence that surrounded the column and broke the lock on the door that led to an interior stairway.

The package was still in its niche at the top of the stairs. Stan tore at the wrappings and pulled its teeth, then crushed the package in his hands. That was the end of...

There was the sound of racing footsteps up the winding stairwell.

HE flattened himself against the wall until they came into view, then launched himself down the stairs, landing squarely on the chest of a burly man so they both rolled down the steep flight of stairs.

Tanner had finally gotten wind of what was going on, Stan thought sharply. But it was too late to do anything about it now. The invasion had been set; you couldn't stop a fleet once it rolled into motion. The overconfident Thuscans would land—to discover to their shocked surprise that there was organized resistance.

Mr. Ainsworth's "apes" wouldn't be a pushover...

"Bastarde..."

The burly man wasn't alone. There was another at the bottom of the stairs. Stan twisted his body, holding the first Italian in front of him. There was a pistol shot and the sound of a bullet smacking into solid flesh. The man whom Stan held screamed shrilly, his eyes flaring wide.

Then all three of them were down. Stan leaped for the door and slammed it after him. A moment later he was sprinting through the low midway of tumbled arches and forlorn columns of the glory that had once been Rome.

He caught another taxicab by the Coliseum, slipped the driver the contents of his wallet, and sagged against the cushions exhausted.

A shot shattered the rear window of the cab and he felt vainly in his coat pocket for his heater. It must have fallen out during the long fall down the flight of stairs, he thought. Which meant that he was defenseless.

He left the cab a few doors down from the alley and sprinted into the darkness, another shot whistling past his ear. He was almost up to the circle of shining black when the bullet plowed into the fleshy part of his back and he half stumbled, half fell into the pool of whirling blackness...

CHAPTER TWELVE

"You didn't succeed, Martin. Come on—wake up so I can tell it to your face. You and the rest of the apes have lost forever!"

He stirred and gagged and then rolled on his side, feeling the pain from his shoulder lance through his body. There had been the shot and he had felt himself falling and then there had been a voice...

Tanner's voice.

His eyes jerked wide open and he sat up, wincing at another flash of pain.

"Finally awake, are you?"

He turned. Tanner was on the small pedestal that held the hoop, standing nonchalantly in front of the circle of whirling black.

"You'll be sorry you woke up, Martin. Frankly, I should think you would be wishing you were dead." He half smiled to himself. "There's knives in the kitchen, incidentally, in case you should want to do something about it. I imagine you have quite a guilt complex."

Stan whipped his head around to look at the small box-like machine that kept score of the fusion packages. Only one light was still lit.

The light for Chicago.

Tanner smiled lightly. "Don't think you've won just because there's only one light left. Fifty fusion packages was our safety factor. We actually only needed one."

Stan's face mirrored what he thought and Tanner read the look.

"That's right," he nodded. "Only one. We wanted to create panic and one will do that. When it goes off, that's all we need. The rest of the world will hear about it seconds later. And then the flight will be on." He paused. "You don't think that people—anywhere—are going to remain in their cities, do you? All the police, all the commissars in existence, couldn't make them do that. And then the air fleets will spring into action. One fleet because it demands vengeance, and the other because the only defense is a good offense, as the ape politicians are so fond of saying."

He shrugged. "You see? It really only takes one for disaster."

Stan gathered his muscles for one last lunge...

Tanner caught the movement—and raised his eyebrows.

"You wouldn't want to do that, Martin. For one reason, I've got Avis. And for another, it would be too late. The blast went off ten seconds ago."

He waved and stepped into the blackness.

Stan reeled over to the set and dialed Chicago. The sheet of blackness formed, wavered, and then faded back to the edges of the hoop.

He had lost, Stan thought, dazed. The city he had been born and raised in was one with the drifting atoms of the air.

Tanner had won, completely. And Tanner had Avis.

Stan huddled in the center of the room, his mind a melee of flickering thoughts. Then a noise at the window caught his ear. The noise of doors slamming and the starting of a thousand automobiles and people running through the streets. He didn't bother to look—he knew what it was.

The exodus of a billion people from ten thousand towns and cities was on the way.

There was six hours to go before the start of the brief, abortive war. Six hours before the air fleets would arrive at their destination.

A day later the Thuscan fleet would settle from the skies to begin the mopping up operation, the operation that would change the face of a green, water world to a world that would be another colony planet for Thusca.

A world in which the human race would play no part.

And there was the matter of the girl...

THE noise outside the street was a steady roar, now. The street was gorged with people on foot and on bicycles and in automobiles, fighting to get out of the city. He could hear screams and curses and over all, the faint crackle of flames.

In a few hours, the city would be a roaring inferno, he thought. There would be nobody left behind to put out the fires. And the scene would be duplicated a thousand times over before the sun went down.

And the next day there would be the final, terrible tempest when the Thuscans arrived. When humanity would go out in a short, confused struggle.

There was nothing left to do but prepare to die...

Then he thought again of Avis and knew there was one last, forlorn chance.

He raced back to the communications room and pressed the switches on the small television set with which he and Tanner used to communicate with Mr. Ainsworth on the Thuscan flagship.

Avis had mentioned that her own fleet was standing by. A small fleet perhaps, but certainly not one without possibilities.

He waited a moment for the tubes to warm up, then dialed the frequency Avis had once mentioned. There was a pause and the screen grew bright. A face wavered on it for a moment and then grew steady. It was the face of a middle-aged man dressed in a dull blue uniform. His eyes looked like they had seen all there was to see of both heaven and hell.

Stan explained the situation urgently. The face nodded acceptance of what had happened.

"Can you get out of the city?"

The sounds outside were a steady roar now. Stan hesitated a moment, then said yes.

"We'll try to pick you up. Take the main artery out of the city to the small wooded park."

"What are you going to do?"

The lines in the man's face deepened. "Outside of picking you up, there's nothing we can do."

Stan flicked off the switch and started for the door. So there was nothing they could do. Nothing they could do to save a world or to save Avis.

Well, that remained to be seen.

HE opened the street door and was almost swept into the tightly packed, fast moving throng. He stepped back into the doorway for a moment, letting the fighting, struggling mob sweep by. A father held a squawking baby high above his head. A woman was crying, hugging a small bundle of clothes to her as she struggled on. Suddenly she slipped and fainted and slid beneath the thousand feet of the mob. Stan didn't see her reappear.

He closed the door and ran to the back. The alley was crowded but not nearly so packed as the street.

Perhaps half an hour had passed since Tanner had appeared in the hoop, he thought. He had five-and-a-half hours to go before the bombs started dropping.

His back pained him and he could feel the blood start to well where he had been shot. He grimaced and struggled on.

A man next to him was lugging a small, portable radio and Stan could hear the frightened announcer reading off the government's mobilization orders and exhortations to remain calm.

They were useless, Stan thought bitterly. They could have no more effect on the tidal waves of humanity leaving its cities than Xerxes had on the ocean, when he had ordered it to be whipped. Humanity was leaving its huddling places and there was nothing that could stop them.

An hour later and he made two miles through the packed outskirts of the city. The crowd was thinning now and he thought he could make out the wooded sections of the park, not more than three of four blocks ahead. It couldn't be too much longer, he thought. He wasn't sure of how much more he could take...

His shirt was torn and the wound in his back was bleeding freely. Worse than that had been the sights he had seen on the way—women and children trampled underfoot, and the few neurotic souls who had given up and taken the short way out by leaping from windows.

It was slaughter, even without the war, he thought. Humanity was destroying itself in senseless panic. And then he was in the wooded area that had grown close to the city. He pushed through the brush and trees until he found a small clearing. The mass of people streamed past it, anxious to put miles between themselves and the buildings that so obviously spelled destruction.

He had waited for perhaps an hour when a small life boat rocket put down in the clearing. He looked at his watch before stepping aboard.

Time had narrowed to three hours.

CHAPTER THIRTEEN

THE war rockets from Avis' home system of Aurelia stretched through space like a thin, red string. There were more than a hundred there, Stan thought, but he knew without asking that they were hopelessly outnumbered by the Thuscan ships.

The small rocket maneuvered over the lead ship—a hatch slid back—and the rocket settled slowly through the opening.

A moment later and Stan was in the main cabin, facing half a dozen tired looking men wearing the same dull blue uniform as the man on the screen. They were supposed to be fighting men, Stan thought, but they didn't look the part.

They looked more like frightened civilians who had been drafted.

The man Stan had seen on the screen introduced himself as Elal and smiled wryly.

"We're not the professionals you've associated with until lately, Martin. Fighting is something new for us. It will be a while before we achieve the hardened look of the warrior race."

His voice was soft and tired. The voice of a man who had lost his spirit, who had ceased to hope.

"What's the situation?" Stan asked.

Elal shrugged. "You should have been able to size it up quickly. We are outnumbered—about ten to one, I would say. We had been hoping until the last minute that perhaps Avis would succeed, that she would be able to prevent the subversion of the planet."

"Just what would that have accomplished?"

74

"You Terrans are not without the means of defense," Elal pointed out. "In many ways you may be backward and primitive but you have deadly weapons. And a planet, strongly organized for resistance, would be very difficult for the Thuscans to take over. They have never succeeded in storming one outright. They have always had to rely on infiltration."

"Your weapons aren't puny either," Stan said. "You have the time fields."

"They have limited application—they are good for only small fields and only for short times. And the Thuscans have neutralizers."

Another man, who looked oddly familiar, spoke up.

"What's happened to Avis?"

Her father, Stan guessed shrewdly.

"She was captured by Tanner."

There was a short silence and the men looked oddly helpless.

"Well, what are you going to do?" Stan burst out. "You're the only hope that's left!"

Elal shrugged. "What is there to do? We have you. Perhaps you will be of help, if you can remember much of Thusca. So far as we know, you are the only man who has been there and returned. Outside of…" And then he broke it off.

"You're going to let the world go by default?" Stan asked coldly. "And Avis, too?"

The group of Aurelian's looked annoyed. "What would you have us do?" Elal asked. "We gambled and we lost. We are outnumbered ten to one. And this is not the only world we have to worry about, Martin. There are a thousand others."

"And you'll be outnumbered at each one, won't you?" Stan asked grimly. "You'll always be retreating but the odds will never get any better. As your ring of defenses collapses and allows you to concentrate more and more, the area the Thuscans have to concentrate on will be steadily getting smaller. You have to make a stand for it—why not here?"

"It wouldn't work. We would lose. And we're far too large a part of our total fleet to take the risk."

They wanted to give up because it looked bad on paper, Stan thought. They didn't want to see blood spilled, they didn't want to get their fingers dirty.

"Where's the Thuscan fleet?"

The young man at the controls worked the dials of a screen, which lit up to a luminous black. There was the Earth at one end of the screen—a green globe the size of a basketball—and then the star-flecked, velvet sky.

Stan watched a small collection of brilliant lights move slowly across the screen. The operator pressed another button and that segment of the heavens suddenly leaped forward into the viewscreen. The collection of lights swiftly evolved into the glowing, rod-like ships of the Thuscans. They were arranged into a triangle, a large, reddish colored ship at the apex.

Mr. Ainsworth would be on that ship, Stan thought. Mr. Ainsworth and Mr. Malcolm and maybe even Tanner.

It was…logical that Tanner would be there. His work on Earth was done. And it was probable that Avis was on the ship with him. She would be valuable as a hostage.

He stared thoughtfully at the screen. It wasn't a neat triangle; it wasn't a really militaristic formation. The files of ships were a little straggly, as if their commanders weren't really expecting any opposition. From any quarter.

"We could go down," Stan said thoughtfully. "We could force the lead ship to land in Europe. It would be Exhibit A; it would stop the war. You would have time to make explanations and if I know the...apes...they wouldn't be such pushovers after that."

"You think it would succeed?" one of the men asked sarcastically.

"There's always the element of surprise," Stan said bitingly. "It's probably the last thing they would be expecting you to do." He paused. "You say that you are outnumbered and your weapons are not the best. Have you ever tried the oldest one of all—courage?"

There was a dead silence.

"You're being very inspirational," Elal said after a moment. "But I don't think you're being very practical."

Stan glanced around the compartment. The pilot was young. He looked expectant, and somewhat hopeful. He would be willing to dare, Stan thought. The others had never fought a war, they didn't know how.

Stan turned to the pilot. "Take it down—towards the lead ship in the Thuscan Fleet!"

"How do we know he's changed?" a voice bleated. "Maybe he's still in league with Thusca!"

Stan turned, the blue of a heat gun shining in his fist. "I have no time to argue—but it's not true." To the pilot: "Take it down!"

"You forget that I'm the leader here," Elal said quietly.

"You've abdicated your position," Stan said softly. "A leader is a man who can lead. You can't. *I* can." His eyes blazed.

"We're going down!"

CHAPTER FOURTEEN

THEY plummeted through space toward the lead ship in the Thuscan fleet that was circling ever closer to the planet below. Stan glanced at his watch. Barely an hour remained before the planet below would be fighting a hideous, futile battle.

Barely an hour left in which he had to accomplish the impossible.

"Look!" somebody shouted. "Look at the screen!"

Stan glanced at it briefly. There was the Thuscan fleet laid out below—much nearer now—and the small, flashing dot that represented his own craft.

Behind him, strung out like a lazy figure C, was the rest of the Aurelian fleet. They were following the leader down, even though they recognized the enormous odds at which they were going to be fighting.

Courage, Stan thought, feeling something catch in his throat. The unknown weapon.

But just how much could it accomplish?

"Contact in half a chrono," the pilot said.

Stan walked over to him.

"Show me how this works."

It was simple enough, Stan discovered. The firing studs for the different, directional rockets could be played like the keys of a piano. And the radar that indicated distance from another object was accurate to the yard.

Stan studied the pilot for a minute, trying to guess at his reflexes. "When we make contact, do exactly as I tell you."

He shifted his gaze to the viewscreen. The Thuscan fleet was much nearer now, but the formation was changing slightly. The triangle was more ragged, more uncertain looking. They weren't sure of what was going to happen, Stan thought, and they were worried.

Which was just what he wanted.

"You'll kill us all!" a voice behind him screamed.

"Maybe I will," Stan mused softly. "I don't promise you a thing…" They were brief miles away now.

"Fire left!"

The port rockets lifted the ship slightly and they flashed directly over the Thuscan lead rocket, a bare half-mile beneath them. The wash from Stan's rockets flared lightly over the Thuscan ship and then they were pulling away.

"Try again."

The pilot turned the rocket in a circle and headed back. Beneath them, the lead Thuscan ship was belching flame and breaking out of formation, trying desperately to get away from the insane men who were bent on committing suicide.

Stan flashed them again, even closer. There was no place for the Thuscan ship to go but down.

STAN laughed outright and drove it like a dog herding sheep, hounding them too close for them to bring their weapons into play, and daring death every time he drove at them.

He was courting death and he knew it. And didn't care. The minutes were ticking slowly by and he knew that time was running out for half a billion people on the green globe below.

He glanced again at the viewscreen. Space was a tangle of flaring lights and rocket trails. But confused as the picture was, he knew one thing. Surprise and courage had been the elements they needed.

They were winning.

He turned to Elal. "Get the Thuscans on the viewscreen."

A moment later, the picture on the screen faded and another control cabin faded in. The creature in the picture recognized Stan and a moment later the sober face of Mr. Ainsworth was staring out at him.

"You shouldn't be doing this, Stan," Mr. Ainsworth said, his voice sounding bewildered and hurt. "Is this the way you pay back friendship? Is this how you repay hospitality?"

He could listen to the words and know they were lies. He could look at Mr. Ainsworth and know what lay beneath that saint's face. But he still wanted to believe. He wanted desperately to believe. To be told by Mr. Ainsworth that all was forgiven.

His throat was dry and he was dripping sweat. His conditioning wasn't going to disappear overnight, he knew. It would be a battle all the time. And this was just the first round.

"I'm going to force down your ship and kill you," he said quietly. "But first, we're going to play tag over every civilized capital on the globe. We're going to let them know just what the story is. And then, if the Thuscan fleet still wants to come in, they can go ahead and try it. But I wouldn't advise it, Ainsworth! The apes won't be easy pickings!"

He flicked off the set. They were in the atmosphere now and the air was screaming past the hull. He could feel the temperature inside the cabin rise and then the refrigeration went into action.

They rocketed over the ocean and then they were over London, a bare five miles up. The ships and their exhaust were clearly visible to the frightened millions camping outside the city.

Stan drove the Thuscans over Paris and Moscow and Tokyo and Washington, timing his rocket blasts and forcing them whichever way he wanted them to go. He threatened to crash them from above if they tried to leave, and threatened to ram them from below if they tried to land.

Governments watched, frightened at the scene and realized what must be waiting out in space. Huge planes that had been winging over arctic wastes and across vast stretches of sea suddenly got crackling messages that forced them to turn abruptly in their courses and head for the nearest air field—whether it was friend or late enemy.

Far out in space, the void was filled with hulled ships and flaring rockets that suddenly mushroomed into gigantic explosions. Down below, Stan drove the Thuscan ship around the world and then toward Europe again.

He finally forced it to crash-land in the Tiergarten in evacuated Berlin.

HIS own ship landed a block away.

The dazed officers in the compartment looked at him for guidance and he realized that he was still the leader—that they still didn't quite know what to do.

"You'll go out that airlock and you'll fight them," he said crisply. "Hand to hand, if you have to. But you'll have to fight them—and you'll have to kill them." He strode to the airlock. "Good luck!"

There was no motion about the other rocket and he thought for a frightening moment that everybody on board had been killed. Then he realized that they were waiting for him to make a move, to show himself for an easy target.

He found a hiding place behind a bit of rubble and adjusted the stud on his heat gun.

They weren't going to stay in their ship long, he thought. He would *make* them come out.

He turned the stud to high and aimed the gun at a port near the control room. The crystal in the port colored, glowed, and suddenly fused. Stan could dimly make out the control console and flashed his heater at that. The violet beam touched the controls and they turned red and fused. Then the beam caught a thin fuel line in the console and there was a sudden spurt of white heat.

Seconds later, the fuel tanks erupted with a roar that showered bits of red hot metal over the whole area.

A moment more, he thought…The air about him was suddenly thick with lancing, violet beams and he felt one touch him lightly on the shoulder, crisping the flesh and setting his shirt on fire. He winced and beat out the flames, keeping an eye on the hatch.

Then the hatch flew open and figures boiled out.

The slaughter was brief, and very thorough. But of all the creatures that boiled out of the hatch, Stan didn't see the two he was looking for.

When it was all over, he walked out to the field and glanced at the bodies. There were none that looked like Tanner or—thank heavens—Avis.

He was touching one body gingerly with his foot when the young pilot ran up to him.

"There was no action on the other side of the ship, was there, sir?"

"No. Why?"

"One of the ports, sir—fused. And there were no flames near it..."

Stan started running for the other side of the ship. There was the blasted port and then footsteps in the carbonized grass that had been flamed when the ship had landed. He ran quickly over the grass, following the footsteps, then glanced ahead into the city.

He caught one, brief glimpse of them. Two figures disappearing behind some rubble, running toward one of the side streets...

And the hoop that Stan knew was in an alley behind the Russian owned and operated department store in the Eastern sector.

Stan dashed through the streets. They were two blocks ahead of him—Tanner and a girl, whom he was half pushing, half pulling.

A beam flared above Stan's head and he ducked and zigzagged from one side of the street to the other.

The figures turned a corner and Stan fired one last, futile shot at them.

When he finally turned into the street, there was nobody in sight—only the whirling black velvet of the hoop.

He hesitated and then dove through it…

…to a street he had seen once before. The Street of Lepers in Casablanca.

The street was deserted—there were no signs of either Tanner or Avis. He walked slowly down the street, and then there was a rustling noise behind them. He whirled, just in time to see Tanner and Avis disappear into the hoop again.

He ran and plunged in after them. It was going to be difficult, he thought. He would have to leave the vicinity of the hoop to look for them. And once his back was turned, they would be going through the hoop once more.

HE caught a quick glimpse of Tanner in the deserted streets of Barcelona, Spain. He almost ran into the two in the empty streets of Shanghai. Madrid, Paris, Stuttgart, Leningrad, Los Angeles, Dallas—the cities flashed by like a deck of cards that was flicked past his eyes. The unending succession of black velvet hoops through which he moved like a man traveling through an infinity of dimensions…

And then the apartment in Bristol and Tanner was there, waiting for him. Simply standing against a table, waiting. Avis was in the far corner, her face frightened and drawn.

Stan paused, eyeing the situation.

"It's been quite a chase, hasn't it?" Tanner asked.

Still the urbane Mr. Tanner, Stan thought.

"I caught you, though, didn't I?"

"It all depends on how you look at it. Perhaps *I've* caught *you.*"

Tanner held an unfamiliar weapon in his hand. Stan looked at it curiously and then knew exactly what it was.

83

Tanner had gotten hold of Avis' time pistol. He was going to kill him like William Clark had been killed.

Tanner was going to age him a hundred years in a second.

"Think you'll get away with it, Tanner?"

"Why not? There's nobody to stop me!"

How many times had he died in the last eight years? Stan wondered. How many times had his life been hanging by a thread, waiting for somebody to cut it?

"Stan! Duck!"

Tanner had been distracted just long enough by the shout. Stan dropped to the carpet and rolled against Tanner's legs. Then they were both on the floor. Stan grabbed for the arm that still clung to the time pistol. Tanner grunted and twisted and then...

Stan paled and almost gagged.

Tanner was flickering.

In the background, Avis screamed. And then Mr. Ainsworth was looking at him.

"I'm your friend," the creature said weakly.

Stan weakened and almost let go. "I'm your friend," the creature repeated softly, triumphantly. "I saved your life, didn't I?"

He was lying in the alley again, back in Chicago, lying there hurt and bleeding. And Mr. Ainsworth had come up to help him. Out of all the millions of people in the city, it was only Mr. Ainsworth who had helped.

"I'm your friend," the creature purred again.

That still, quiet morning when the chill air had hung heavy over the city...

And then the conditioning was totally gone and Stan felt exultant. He hadn't realized...

He gripped the arm harder and twisted and the time pistol went skittering across the carpet.

Mr. Ainsworth looked surprised and faded back into Tanner. A powerful, cold-eyed Tanner who suddenly wrenched free and bent Stan under him. He reached for a water carafe from the table to bring it down to smash Stan's skull.

Stan jerked his head to one side and doubled his legs under him and lashed out with them, catching Tanner in the chest. Tanner staggered backwards towards the hoop, his foot unintentionally pressing the on switch. The circle of black started to build up.

The time pistol was only a few feet away. Stan snatched at it and turned it on the still reeling Tanner. It caught the creature flush at the same time as he toppled back through the black velvet circle.

Stan's last glimpse of The Enemy was of a suddenly very old and aging man—hair whitened and thinning, lines etched deeply in the face, clothes sagging limply from a suddenly shriveled frame—toppling backwards into the hoop.

And then the solid circle of black suddenly broke and faded into the frame again.

Stan turned on his side and got sick. The Bristol hoop had been tuned to Chicago. Only there was no more Chicago and no more hoop there. But Tanner had toppled through—to where?

The creature that had been Mr. Ainsworth and Tanner was lost in a space that had no beginning and no end.

And no exit.

CHAPTER FIFTEEN

THEY stood on a parapet of the first building to be erected in New Chicago and watched the tiny flares of the workmen who had come from all over the world to rebuild the city. It was night—a cool, almost clear night with only a few faint clouds scudding across the face of the full moon. The stars blazed down, a million tiny candles flickering against a background of black.

Avis moved her head a fraction and said: "Do you love me?"

"What do you think?"

After a moment, she said: "I have to go back tomorrow."

"I know."

"I...don't want to leave."

"Why not?"

She smiled in the darkness. "You know why not. I don't want to leave you."

He hunkered down on the parapet and she sat down beside him. "They never told you my last name, did they?" she asked suddenly.

"It's Tanner, isn't it?"

"He was my brother."

He waited a moment, then asked: "What happened to him?"

"He wanted power," she said quietly. "Our society wouldn't give it to him. So he sold out. Of his own free will—he hadn't been conditioned like you were." She paused. "I suppose as long as there's a human race, there will be people who want power and who will be willing to sell their fellow man to get it."

Stan frowned. "That's why they sent you down to try and stop him, wasn't it?"

She nodded. "I was the most qualified." Pause. "A Thuscan eventually took his place, I know. But I wonder how he actually died. Did you ever hear about him on Thusca?"

"He died a hero," Stan lied.

She smiled in the dark. "Thanks anyway. But I knew him, too."

"They used him as a model," Stan said. "Like Mr. Ainsworth and Mr. Malcolm. There actually were human beings like that. Somewhere along the line, the Thuscans captured them and studied them so they could imitate them. Ainsworth and Malcolm and your brother served as models." He shuddered. "Perhaps on some world there's an imitation Stanley Martin walking around."

They watched the stars for a while and then Avis said: "You're a strong man, Stan. How did they ever...break you?"

"A simple technique—brainwashing you could call it. The Thuscans set up Mr. Malcolm and Mr. Ainsworth and I was the man between. Mr. Malcolm was the enemy; Mr. Ainsworth was the friend. Mr. Ainsworth would 'rescue' me from Mr. Malcolm. There's no quicker way to build up a friendship, I felt obligated, in a sense. And then there was torture...and machines. When my memory came back, I thought I had it all figured. I only made one mistake. I never thought Tanner was a Thuscan."

"He fooled a lot of people, including myself. You shouldn't feel bad."

"But I do! If Tanner had been a real human being, then they would never have needed me...Clever psychologists though they were, they had to work through a human agency as a safety factor. If Tanner had been real, they could have done it through him."

"You broke the conditioning," she pointed out. "How?"

He smiled. "That morning when they jumped me. They beat me up for half an hour and nobody came to my rescue. Nobody but Ainsworth. Even in Chicago, people don't stand by and let a 17-year-old kid get killed by three men. Tanner had used the time pistol. What had seemed to take a half-hour for me actually occurred in seconds. Nobody could have helped me if they had wanted to."

HE stared moodily at the sky. "You know, there isn't much here for me, Avis. I lost my whole family when Chicago was wiped off the map. Larry had died before then, of course." He lowered his voice to a brooding sadness. "And the indoctrination I had, it hasn't entirely worn off. Sometimes I think of people as…apes again."

"What do you want to do, Stan?" Her voice was cautious.

He stood up and waved at the sky.

"I'm going back with you! There's a thousand worlds up there I've never seen, a thousand adventures I've never had. And there's still Thusca…"

She laughed softly. "Anything else?"

He ran his fingers through her hair and brushed her lips. "You know better than that…"

"We leave tomorrow," she repeated after a moment.

He kissed her softly and then lay back on the parapet and stared at the flickering stars overhead. A breeze came in off the lake and tugged at his hair and he imagined it sweeping on, blowing to a thousand worlds he had never seen.

And a thousand adventures he had never had…

THE END

If you've enjoyed this book, you will not want to miss these terrific titles...

A BACK DOOR TO ETERNITY...

There were eight of them—four men and four women—and some of them were running from the law. Random chance brought them to the mountaintop cabin of Eli Thornbolt, a reclusive scientist whose scientific dreams needed money to become a reality.

But when his guests walked through the back door of his cabin, they soon found themselves on an incredible journey through the vast depths of outer space, to a brave new world—a world whose actual formation was spawned by the very entrance of their spacecraft into that region of the galaxy.

Join these unwitting space pioneers in their struggles as they fly through space to destinations unknown, and join them as they strive to survive on an unknown planet whose location was a complete mystery!

CAST OF CHARACTERS

DAVE MARLIN
He was an ex-con with no money and nowhere to go…What could he do but follow his instincts?

SALLY CAMINO
A slick floozy on the run from the law, but hiding from the cops in a spaceship isn't always the best idea!

LEN MCGRUDER
Just an ex-cop who played dirty and wasn't afraid to sell his best friend down the river.

PEARL
Just because she was prophetic didn't mean she could tell them where they were going…or why.

BART DUCHANE
Nice on the surface, shady underneath, he spent much of his time trying to stay ahead of the law.

ELI THORNBOLT
He was just a bit off his rocker, and he didn't expect his own invention to behave with a purpose of its own!

SLINKY LINK
This parasitic type of petty criminal was not particularly dangerous—not particularly anything.

LOOK TO THE STARS

By
WILLARD HAWKINS

ARMCHAIR FICTION
PO Box 4369, Medford, Oregon 97504

For more information about Armchair Books and products, visit our website at…

www.armchairfiction.com

Or email us at…

armchairfiction@yahoo.com

The sky is filled with lonely stones—planets waiting for the first
breath of life to warm them.
N'urth was such a world—and the Gods smiled on it.

"TELL me, my queen mother, the story of the gods."

"Do you never tire, son, of those ancient legends? But no—let this not seem a reproof. It is well that a prince of the royal line should ponder much on those mighty ones, who came from the sun, where dwells El-Leighi, the source of all, to create a fair world—the world in which some day you will reign. Shall I speak, then, of Solin-Ga-Ling, patron of husbandry and Lord of the North, or would you hear of the gentle Maha-Bar-Astro, sweet goddess who fashions the dreams of childhood? Or would you know of the mysterious Noor-Ah-Mah, who died twice, lived thrice, and was both male and female by turns?"

"Tell me of them all; but first, mother, who was the mightiest of the gods?"

"Hush, child! Among beings so exalted it would be presumptuous for mortals to regard one above the other. But know this—for it concerns you and your pride of race:

Splendid legends relate to the strength and virtues of Maha-Ra-Lin, Lord of the South, sometimes called the Life-giver. For it was he who created Noor-Ah-Mah from a rock by the sea, and breathed his own life into her nostrils."

"But, mother, was he not defeated in battle?"

"It was a battle beyond our understanding—of forces that we cannot comprehend, and for a purpose beyond our knowledge—though it is said that in some manner the strife arose over the sex to be awarded the newly created Noor-Ah-Mah. Maha-Ra-Lin would have endowed the partly formed being with the attributes of a god, but Bar-Doo-Chan, Lord of the West, contended for a goddess. In their mighty clash of wills, the heavens were rent with lightning, the seas were churned, mountains were heaved by the all-powerful ones across the land. Legend has it that a single moon shone from the heavens before that event, but a lightning bolt hurled by Maha-Ra-Lin at his antagonist failed of its mark. It smote *the moon by chance, splitting the heavenly body in twain, so that two moons now circle the continents of N'urth."*

"Then Bar-Doo-Chan, who defeated Maha-Ra-Lin, was the mightiest."

"Nay, that you must not say. True, at the end of three days Maha--Ra-Lin acknowledged himself defeated. Yet it is written that he nobly abandoned the fray out of pity for the helpless creatures of N'urth, and for the newly created Noor-Ah-Mah, knowing that if the battle continued they would all be destroyed. And so Noor-Ah-Mah became a goddess, and in that aspect she is depicted by our sculptors as a mighty huntress, running with upraised spear cheek-by-cheek with Bar-Doc-Chan; But Maha-Ra-Lin, the Life-giver, could not wholly undo his original design, so that at times she reverted to the form of a male. That is why, in ancient carvings, we sometimes find Noor-Ah-Mah pictured as a god, carrying lightnings of destruction in his clenched hand."

"Then, after all, Maha-Ra-Lin was the greatest?"

"He was a mighty being, son. Yet how can any be considered greater than Pi-Ruh-Al, to whom even the other gods and goddesses turned for counsel? Pi-Ruh-Al, the great mother, goddess of beauty, of wisdom, creator of mortal life…"

CHAPTER ONE

THE rain settled into a steady downpour. Drenched to the marrow, Dave Marlin struggled on through the darkness and mire. At times he stumbled away from the wagon trail and floundered through sodden verdure that tangled his feet, clutched with slimy tendrils at his clothing, or lashed his face. Occasionally he stopped to curse the road, the darkness, the storm; again to heap maledictions on the truck driver who had dumped him off on this byway to nowhere.

He should have kept to the paved highway. A light blinking through the rain, seemingly not far up the mountainside, had lured his feet. It had long since been lost to view, yet he struggled on. The trail surely must lead somewhere, even if only to a deserted sawmill or mine shaft.

His feet slipped and he went down cursing. As he struggled out of the puddle, gouging grit and slime from eyes and nostrils, he became aware of a deeper black looming ahead.

It was the rear of an old-style open roadster. Through the swish of waters his ears caught the sound of hammering on metal.

Feeling his way along the side, he came to a man who was muttering to himself with bitter emphasis while doing things to the engine under the upraised hood.

"Trouble, buddie?" demanded Marlin.

The other jerked up his head so suddenly that it struck the hood. He snarled an epithet; then: "Who the devil?"

"Just a wayfarer," Marlin answered. "Just a wayfarer, buddie, out for a stroll on this beautiful moonlit evening."

"Layoff the comedy!" snarled the other, again diving under the hood. "And get goin' if you can't help."

"Why don't you turn on the lights?"

"Because she ain't got no lights—that's why."

"Battery dead?" asked Marlin. Receiving no answer, he edged back to the instrument panel. As he started searching beneath it for possible ends of disconnected wires, he became aware of a squirming movement under the hand, which rested on the seat.

"Take your paws off me, you slimy fish!" came a tense feminine voice. When he made no move to comply, the figure, which had been slumped down, in the seat became a sudden bundle of fury.

"Easy, sister!" he protested, deftly capturing the small hands in his muscular grasp. "No use getting excite—" He paused. "What's this? Iron bracelets?"

The other man sloshed toward him threateningly. "Get out of what ain't none of your business!" he snapped. "You was headin' up the road. Just keep goin'—and you'll stay outta trouble."

Marlin felt the slender wrists grow tense within his grasp. The short length of chain connecting the handcuffs tinkled.

"Sorry, bo," he said softly. "The lady's jewelry intrigues me."

A hard object pressed sharply into his side. "Scram!"

With panther-like quickness, Marlin twisted. The gun barked as his arm knocked it away. Then the two were down in the sodden grass, flailing and squirming for advantage.

Either because he was the stronger or because luck favored him in the slippery rough-and-tumble, Marlin arose with the automatic in his possession.

"This," he commented, "is better. I've never been good at taking orders." He considered a moment. "If the car won't start, it won't. That leaves two courses open to us. We can sit and wait till some one comes along—which isn't likely—or we can hoof it until we come to something better. I saw a light up beyond."

"I'm tired of sitting in the car," the girl put in. "Anything's better than freezing here."

"Maybe you don't know, smart guy," her companion growled, "that you're tangling with the law." He tapped his chest.

"Detective—eh?"

"Yeah," the girl cut in, "and don't forget to tell him about your phony stunt—kidnapping me across the state line without extradition papers."

Marlin studied them for a moment. He had no desire to run up against the law. But if this officer was out of his jurisdiction—

"I get it," he said. "You're pulling something shady—that's why you tried to make it on this back trail. All right, brother—take off the jewelry."

Grudgingly, the detective removed the handcuffs.

"Try any funny stuff," he observed, "and it'll go hard with the both of you. This is Sally Camino," he informed Marlin. "Wanted for workin' a con game. I can turn her over to the authorities here if I have to. Won't be no trouble to get extradition papers. I'm just tryin' to save the state money."

"What's your name?" demanded Marlin.

"Len McGruder. What you so nosey for?"

"Just getting acquainted. Mine's Dave Marlin. Come on, Sal. Any baggage?"

"This jerk wouldn't even give me a chance to pack a toothbrush," she returned vindictively.

Fortunately, she was dressed in slacks. After a futile attempt to negotiate the mud in her high-heeled shoes, she left them sticking in the ooze.

"I'll take it barefooted," she observed philosophically.

Less from chivalry than curiosity, Marlin helped her when she stumbled and assisted her over the deeper puddles. He decided, in the process, that she was firm-fleshed and well formed. After the first few yards she refused his help.

"Keep your muddy paws off of me!" she snapped. "You too!" as McGruder attempted to thrust his bulk between them.

They plodded on through the mud and drizzle. The road climbed upward at an agonizing grade. Marlin no longer cursed. In the presence of companions in misery, he became tauntingly ironical. It was they who were buffeted and tormented—he was the strong man, unaffected by the elements, able to "take it."

"We shoulda stayed in the car," growled McGruder.

"Only room for two of us," returned Marlin. "Want to go back with me, Sal?"

"Not if I know what I'm doing!" the girl snapped, brushing a lock of wet hair out of her eyes.

Topping a steep rise, they came unexpectedly upon the shelter.

CHAPTER TWO

A light gleamed feebly through a small window. Closer approach revealed that it was set in a wall, which formed the front of a dwelling partly extending back into the cliff.

They pressed their faces against the dripping pane. Beside a fireplace in which a few dying embers glowed faintly, a robust man with a flowing beard was nodding over a book. A kerosene lamp flickered on the table beside him.

They felt along the wall for a door and rapped. After a moment, it opened. The beard was thrust forward and the man behind it stood regarding them from beneath bushy eyebrows.

"We're lost," began Marlin. "What's the chance—?"

"Eh?" the bearded man craned his neck, peering beyond them. "So you're the ones we've been waiting for. Where's the other?"

"There's only the three of us."

With a slightly puzzled manner, he allowed them to enter. Marlin crossed to the fireplace. "Mind if I build this up?"

Not waiting for a reply, he heaped on chunks of pine log from the half-filled woodbox and soon had a rousing fire. McGruder and the girl knelt gratefully in front of the blaze— the girl shivering. Not bad, Marlin decided, at his first sidelong glimpse of her face—or wouldn't be, when her wet hair was fixed up. Then he growled at himself and abruptly turned away.

Their host stood with folded arms, surveying the mud-smeared trio with evident distaste. Experiencing a vague sense of alien presences, Marlin suddenly whirled, his hand clutching at the pocket in which McGruder's automatic reposed.

A door, apparently leading to the interior of the mountain, was partly open. Peering from the narrow aperture were three curiously repellent faces and one of singular beauty.

Sally and the detective, crouching before the fire, turned at his smothered exclamation. The three faced the barrage of eyes in silence until the bearded man gestured peremptorily.

"Shut the door," he ordered. "Come in if you must."

As they trooped into the room, Marlin caught a glimpse of a dark passageway. The unmistakable earthy smell of a mineshaft or tunnel reached his nostrils.

They were a nondescript group. At first glance, three of the newcomers had appeared to be men. Marlin saw now that one was a woman. She had a bulbous nose, bleary red eyes, and a scar that twisted one corner of her mouth into the semblance of a grin. Her gaunt figure was swathed in a dingy robe.

One of the men was powerful and well knit—he looked to be a match for Marlin himself. The other was wizened and under-sized, with a shrewd, weasel face. Strands of greasy hair overhung his eyes, forcing him to cock his head like a poodle in order to see. Both men had made shift to pull their trousers over their underwear before putting in an appearance.

In contrast to these was the fourth—a girl of perhaps eighteen with a sweetly innocent face framed in a shimmering halo of golden hair. In her long white robe she was a vision of ethereal loveliness. The eyes of Marlin and McGruder instinctively fastened upon her.

The woman with the twisted grin cackled. "Look your fill, smarties, for that's all you'll get. Pearl ain't for the likes of you, so don't get ideas."

The weasel-faced man sidled forward, extending a clammy hand. "Wukkum to our dump," he said ingratiatingly. "Meet the gang. My name's Link—Percival B. Link for the blotter, Slinky Link to my frien's." He jerked a thumb toward the woman. "Maw Barstow. This overgrown hunk of meat is Bart DuChane, alias Chaney the Great. Just finished doing a stretch for manslaughter. Oughta stuck to his crystal gazing."

The eyes of the man thus introduced glittered venomously, but his lips forced a smile. He spoke in a controlled voice.

"I might suggest that people who discuss others too freely sometimes meet with accidents."

Marlin studied him with a sense of taking the measure of an adversary. "My name is Dave Marlin," he acknowledged.

"Who's your frien's?" demanded Link.

The detective replied, nodding toward the girl who had worn the handcuffs. "Sally Camino—slickest floozie in the con-game racket. My name's McGruder. D. A.'s office," he added significantly.

Link peered through his thatch of hair. "McGruder," he said reflectively. "Ain't you the Len McGruder that was kicked off the force in Columbus for hijacking? Sure! I know you!"

Marlin swung on the detective. "You're no law officer," he said. "Let's see that badge."

"Keep your hands offa me!" the detective snarled, clutching his coat.

Sally Camino faced him in sudden fury. "You rat!" she spat at him. "You're an even bigger phony than I guessed. Taking me across the state line so's you could put the screws on the gang. Well, let me tell you, fake copper, when Briscoe hears of this—"

"You one of the Briscoe mob?" demanded Link. "Why I was practic'ly lined up with Briscoe—before I got sent up the last time. It's a small world, ain't it?"

The girl glanced at him with repugnance. "Yeah? That just about makes us pals, don't it?"

The irony was wasted. "Sure does," he grinned.

"How about her?" McGruder indicated the golden-haired girl.

"That's Pearl," explained Link. "She ain't all there."

"A lot you know about it!" retorted Maw Barstow. "Pearlie's brighter than you think. Is these the ones that was comin', dearie?" she demanded.

The girl's lips parted in a beatific smile.

"Has vishuns," explained Link. He tapped his forehead to indicate a mysterious form of mental activity. "The old guy—he's nuts too."

This confidence was imparted in a lowered voice, but hardly low enough to avoid being overheard.

"Who is he?" demanded McGruder.

"The name," responded the vibrant voice of the bearded man, "is Elias Thornboldt. And your informant is perfectly correct when he assures you that I am crazy."

The newcomers stared.

"What of it!" Thornboldt demanded, his voice rising in pitch. "I have brains, even if they are addled. I have respectability. I should associate with scientists—decent citizens—instead of scum. Thieves, murderers, pickpockets, harlots—you are not nice people, not any of you!"

He glared at the group as if challenging denial.

"With my brains," he went on, breathing heavily, "I should create a wonderful spaceship—instead of a monstrosity that was never intended on heaven or earth.

Fortunately, I know I am mad. The rest of you do not know what vermin you are!"

Marlin felt a hand plucking at his sleeve. He glanced down to meet the eyes of Link peering through strands of dank hair.

"We better ooze out," the creature said. "When the old gink gets started like that he'll keep it up all night."

The passage, as Marlin had surmised, was a tunnel through the rock. Bart DuChane led the way with a flashlight. A narrow plank walk marked its length for something like a hundred feet. They emerged on what seemed to be a ledge of the open mountainside. The rain was still pouring, but an outcropping overhead partly protected the ledge. Across the way, a rim of tall pines could be discerned against the murky sky.

"It's the hollow of an ancient crater," DuChane volunteered. "That dark mass in the pit below—but why spoil your anticipation? Tomorrow you'll see for yourselves." He laughed unpleasantly. "These are the bunkhouses—ladies to the left, men to the right. Maw is a stickler for the proprieties."

They entered a narrow shack—apparently one of several along the ledge. There were two lower and two upper bunks. Since the lower had been appropriated by DuChane and Link, the late comers climbed into the upper tier.

"Looks almost as if they was expecting us—or somebody," commented McGruder. "The old goof sorta hinted—"

"They were," chuckled DuChane. "You'd be surprised."

CHAPTER THREE

DAVE Marlin stood on the ledge in the chill air of early morning, looking into the sodden depths below. The rain had ceased, but the rays of the newly risen sun as yet had scarcely found their way into the crater.

He turned, shivering, as DuChane sauntered toward him. "What's that thing down below?"

"What does it look like?"

"Like a huge ball of clay. But the scaffolding and building equipment—these bunkhouses—indicate human handiwork. The old duffer said something about a spaceship. This couldn't be—"

"There's little enough I can tell you," responded DuChane. "I've been here less than a week. Slinky and I lost our bearings in a storm. It's a good hideout—and we're seemingly expected to stick around. The dipsomaniac and her queer companion have been here longer. She used to cook for the construction crew.

"Whatever that thing is—" he indicated the huge mud-colored ball in the pit below—"was practically in that condition when we arrived. The self-styled scientist, Thornboldt, seems to have started out with the idea of pioneering in space travel. My information comes chiefly from an article in a scientific magazine that I ran across in his shack, denouncing him as a charlatan. Near as I can gather, he evolved certain theories about nullifying gravity by atomic polarization—if that means anything to you. Claimed to do it by creating violent stresses within a magnetic field. The attacking author—some scientific duck by the name of Lamberton—acknowledged that there was a mathematical basis for Eli's conception, but pointed out that inconceivable power would be required to demonstrate the theory. Do I bore you?"

Marlin started. "Far from it." Then: "You're an educated man," he commented irrelevantly.

Bart DuChane threw back his head and laughed, the sound echoing from the opposite cliffs.

"Same to you," he retorted. "I recognized the Harvard accent. Like old Eli, it is a shame that we should be associating with scum—except that—as he so charmingly puts it—we are scum ourselves." He paused, then, lowering his voice: "Slinky didn't exaggerate. I have engaged in many shady pursuits, not the least of which is bilking the credulous by the ancient and phony art of crystal gazing. The manslaughter rap was the result of a tavern brawl. I have a weakness for low company."

His frankness was a pointed invitation for similar confidences. Marlin hesitated, then, with a shrug: "Not much of interest to tell about myself. My degree isn't from Harvard—nevertheless, it is from a university of good standing. It just happens that there are more openings for a bruiser than a scholar. I wasn't doing so badly in professional football, filling in with wrestling exhibitions and some boxing. Then I fell for a dame—fell hard. A guy without money was mud to her—so I had to get money. Hooked up with a smuggling mob, trucking the stuff over the border. Eventually we had a run-in with revenue officers, and a couple of them were so unfortunate as to stop lead. I got a minimum sentence, but it was plenty long."

"When you got out, naturally, the dame hadn't bothered to wait."

Marlin made no attempt to answer. DuChane nodded.

"It bears out old Goofus. We are not nice people. I wonder what the eighth will be like."

"The eighth?"

"There's to be another, according to legend. You saw the girl, Pearl. It seems she has prophetic spells. According to predictions which Maw claims the girl dropped, eight of us are due to show up, in addition to Eli—four male, four female. What is to happen then is rather vague, but Maw drops dark hints about a mysterious journey. She and Pearl were here first; then came Link and I. Thus you and your friends were more or less expected."

"Surely," expostulated Marlin, "you don't believe—"

"Believe? Without proof, I neither believe nor disbelieve. It's as bigoted to do one as the other. However, we need only one more arrival—female, of course—to complete the prophecy. I hope she turns out to be a good-looker—though I'll admit your friend Sal isn't bad."

Marlin turned away, somehow annoyed.

"Is there such a custom around here as breakfast?"

DuChane sniffed the air. "Maw Barstow seems to have anticipated your question. The eating shack is beyond the bunkhouses."

THE fare produced was abundant if not choice. The whole group evinced hearty appetites, even Pearl, who, despite a soiled ill-fitting gown, seemed scarcely less lovely than she had under the flickering lamplight. She smiled amiably but spoke not at all.

While eating, Marlin let his eyes rove speculatively over the group.

The waif who had crouched beside him, shivering and disheveled, over the fire last night now looked somewhat more the part of an underworld moll. Sally had made an attempt to do her hair, but the dab of color applied to her lips accentuated the wary hardness of her expression.

Len McGruder, bull-necked, furtive-eyed, loose-lipped, inspired in Marlin a deep antipathy. "A man who would sell his best friend down the river," was his mental summation.

Maw Barstow, referred to by DuChane as a dipsomaniac, was probably not as old as she looked. Her unsavory appearance seemed due more to disfigurement than to disposition. A rather sentimental but plainspoken person, she was unquestionably devoted to Pearl.

Slinky Link, with his ingratiating yet repellent manner, was a parasitic type of petty criminal—not particularly dangerous—not particularly anything.

DuChane, as Marlin sensed him, was a man at war with himself. "In a way," reflected Marlin, "he's too much like me."

The thought occurred that if he were looking at himself through other eyes, he would not be more favorably impressed than by the others. "I'd see a poker-faced lug with a cauliflower ear and the body of a stevedore," he reflected. "It'd be pretty hard to guess that a hard-looking egg like me ever dabbled in science and still has a yen to find out what fascinating stuff is hidden in the covers of every book—even if that book is only a human face."

It was difficult to account for the oldster, Elias Thornboldt. Danish, Marlin judged him to be. Apparently he was providing food and shelter for the gathering, much as he despised them all. He sat at the head of the table, coldly aloof, consuming food in enormous mouthfuls.

When his appetite was appeased, Thornboldt stalked from the cook-shack, wiping his mouth with the back of his hand. A few moments later, Marlin found him standing on the ledge, moodily staring down at the huge ball of clay.

"Still it moves!" he muttered. "It moves and rolls and grows."

"What moves?" demanded Marlin sharply. "That thing down there? And what is it?"

The older man turned as if to speak. But he only glared at the group surrounding him and abruptly walked away.

"It's a fact," DuChane commented. "If you watch patiently you can see it. The ball seems to be resting in a bed of ooze—a sort of tarry substance. As the sun rises, it softens under the heat, and when the heat is withdrawn, it hardens. The alternate expansion and contraction seems to impart a rotation to the ball. It's more than a hundred feet across, yet in the time I've been here, I'll swear it's turned half way over. And that isn't all. Care to take a trip down?"

Presently they stood on a precarious scaffolding close to the huge sphere. The bed of ooze could be discerned engulfing its base. Already, under the heat of the sun, a steaming effluvium was rising from the surface. The outside of the ball was caked with a grayish crust of the stuff.

"Feel it," urged DuChane. "Hard?"

"Yes, it's hard," admitted Marlin. "Like stone."

"Now look." DuChane caught up a crowbar and drove it into the bulging wall. It pierced the crust and sank a short distance into the interior.

"Push on it," he directed.

MARLIN tested the resistance to the bar. Under pressure it sank deeper. He could even twist it slowly.

"Seems kind of—rubbery—inside," he commented.

"Pull it out."

He did so. Immediately the hole filled with a flowing exudation similar to the ooze below him. It spread over the edges and began to harden.

"Acts like the stuff they used to put in bicycle tires to make them puncture-proof," commented Marlin. "Is it solid clear through?"

DuChane stared. He was breathing more heavily than his recent exertion seemed to warrant.

"I forgot you don't know. This is Thornboldt's spaceship. Or was. He built it in the form of a metal sphere, girded and braced inside, all equipped with dynamos and machinery. Had a big crew of workmen. When it was just about finished—even provisioned—his backers decided that the whole thing was crazy and shut off his money supply. Articles like that one by Lamberton finished them. To cap the climax, the thing broke through its scaffold and sank into this pit."

"Funny place to build in the first place."

"His idea was to keep the construction a secret from the general public. This crater-like depression, with its only entrance through the old mine tunnel, was far enough out of the way to accomplish the purpose, even though it must have enormously increased the cost of assembling materials. Anyway, after it fell into the pit, the creeping rotation commenced and the shell has gradually taken on this coating of lava—or whatever the stuff is. It's at least four feet thick by this time. Somewhere inside is an entrance port, but there's no way of locating it. The whole thing is so incomprehensible that it's driven him crazy. At least he thinks it has."

"You think otherwise?"

DuChane glanced at his companion. "Possibly his theories are ridiculous, but no one can deny that the ball actually moves and is coating itself with a thick layer of this lava-like stuff. It's just one of those accidental freaks of nature."

Marlin brushed at a swarm of insects and leaned over to follow the flight of a bird into the depths below.

"Two to one it never comes up," DuChane offered. "The stuff is like flypaper. The smell seems to have a fatal attraction for birds and small animals—chipmunks and the like. Or perhaps they're drawn by the seeds that blow in and stick to the surface. Sometimes they escape, but if the consistency is right, it sucks them in, like quicksand. Maw Barstow claims she lost a flock of chicks that way. And if you can believe her, several dogs, and a cat or two, have been trapped by the ooze during her time. There's even a story about some calves and sheep that wandered over the ledge and never could be located, the inference being…"

They were interrupted by the arrival of Thornboldt, followed reluctantly by Link and McGruder. He was carrying pick and shovel and seemed unexpectedly imbued with energy.

"Get tools," he commanded tersely. "You can't stand around here like drones. I have valuable equipment in there. It must be saved."

He attacked the shell with furious strokes of the pick. After a moment, Marlin joined his efforts with the crowbar.

There was no room for the others to participate, even if they had felt inclined to help. They stood watching curiously as Marlin and Eli broke through the crust. This was the easiest part of the undertaking. From a depth of two or three inches below the surface, the substance was a sticky, rubbery mass, which inexorably flowed back to fill the gap made by each blow of pick or crowbar.

"You ain't gettin' nowhere," volunteered Link, peering through his hair.

Eli paused long enough to glare at him. "What would you suggest?" he demanded, then scathingly added, "Loafer!"

"If you had something you could push through. A pipe— or—or something."

The scientist dropped his pick.

"Is it out of the mouths of fools and nit-wits I must get ideas!" he exploded. "Come!"

The rest following, he picked his way over scaffolding, rocks, and heaps of construction material. He stopped, frowningly studying a section of drainpipe some two feet across and five feet long.

"We will try this," he decided.

CHAPTER FOUR

THEY managed to get the cylinder up on the scaffolding and to insert one end in the opening gouged in the outer shell. Slow but steady progress toward penetrating the gummy mass was achieved by imparting a rotary motion to the pipe section. By mid-morning, Marlin had rigged up a crude leverage device of timbers, on the principle of a pipe wrench, which expedite, the process of screwing the cylinder into the interior.

From time to time it was necessary to shovel out the accumulation of ooze. DuChane called Marlin's attention to a dead field mouse in one of the shovel loads.

"No calves?" queried Marlin.

"Not yet, but you can't tell."

By nightfall they had made definite progress. The pipe was buried at least two feet in the sphere. Tired and not a little out of sorts they returned to the cook-shack. "Me, I'm through," growled McGruder. "I'm hittin' the trail first thing tomorrow—and what's more sis, you're comin' with me," he stared at Sally.

"That's what you think!" she responded disdainfully.

But a plentiful breakfast, or perhaps curiosity, altered the detective's plans. When operations were resumed, he showed up tardily to take a hand.

By mid-afternoon, they had succeeded in screwing the pipe some four and a half feet into the interior, when an obstacle was encountered.

Marlin straightened his weary back. "Dig the stuff out," he instructed. "We've struck the shell—I hope."

When the message was relayed to Eli that the shell had been reached, he came plunging through the tunnel.

"Do nothing till I come!" he shouted from the ledge above. With utter disregard for safety, he hurtled down the slope and drew up panting on the platform.

"We will cut through," he announced. "It needs a small man." He looked at Link appraisingly. "Can you handle a blowtorch?"

When the slinky one was safely at work under Marlin's direction, Eli impatiently herded the others away.

"You are doing no good here. Come—help with the things I must take."

The group eyed him with astonishment.

"Take where?" demanded DuChane. "You don't expect this contraption actually to fly?"

"What I think is my own affair!" Thornboldt's beard trembled with the vehemence of his indignation. "Who are you to question my intentions—you who cannot even comprehend my scientific principles!"

With raised eyebrows, DuChane glanced at Marlin. Then, accompanied by McGruder, he followed the scientist up the winding trail while Link continued his blowtorch operations. Whatever the inventor's intentions might be, Marlin felt an insatiable curiosity to view the interior of the incredible sphere.

"Got her!" presently came the muffled announcement from the depths of the pipe. Link wriggled out, holding the blowtorch gingerly at arm's length.

"Melted away like butter," was the little man's comment. "Now a safe I cut into oncet—"

Marlin lost the rest by starting up the hill to lend Sally Camino a hand with a heavy chest she was carrying.

"He's got us all working," she observed, as Marlin took the burden. "We've been packing stuff all morning." Absently she dislodged a pebble from between her bare toes. "What's he going to do, bury himself in that thing?"

"You've got me." Marlin shrugged.

By the time he had deposited the chest on the platform, McGruder and DuChane appeared, carrying a long packing case between them. Maw Barstow followed, also burdened, and after her Eli himself. Smiling serenely, but empty handed, Pearl brought up the rear.

"I must be the first inside," insisted Eli. "Bring the other boxes."

They did not depart until the scientist, heaving and puffing, and by dint of wholehearted shoving on the part of those outside, had managed to squeeze his bulk through the pipe. They heard the sound of rending fabric, accompanied by agonized imprecations, as he worked his way over the jagged metal edges. Then followed a heavy "plop."

"Are you hurt?" Marlin called.

"Naturally I am hurt! I am killed!" came the dark response. "But no matter. Pass me those boxes."

At Marlin's suggestion, Link first crawled through with the blowtorch and trimmed away the jagged metal. Then the boxes were pushed through and they returned for more.

Marlin glanced curiously around Thornboldt's recent living quarters. The shack was nearly stripped. Books, apparatus, provisions, bedding—everything except the larger pieces of furniture—had been packed.

"The old rascal is nuts, all right," was Marlin's comment to Sally. The others had departed with their loads. "Think we've got all he wants?"

Before she could answer, a staccato volley of shots interrupted. The sounds appeared to come from the slope below.

CHAPTER FIVE

BOTH hurried to the single window. Where the wagon trail skirted the base of the rocky hillside, a half dozen crouching figures came into view. Armed with rifles and pistols, they were creeping cautiously up the incline.

A single shot from above caused some of the group to drop flat. Others dodged into the brush. There was a movement among the lengthening shadows at the left.

"What goes on!" demanded Sally. "Gang war?"

"They're not shooting at each other," Marlin asserted, after watching the cautious maneuvers of the two groups. "Looks as if they were closing in on someone. Sheriff's posse, I guess."

Another shot directed their eyes to the rock behind which the fugitive or fugitives must be hiding.

From its concealment, a figure edged into view. There appeared to be only one.

"Poor devil—sure is done for," commented Marlin. "Must be public enemy number one, to judge by the number in the posse. Look! There he goes!"

Crouching close to the ground, the overalled figure dodged from cover to cover, each fleeting appearance bringing a fusillade of shots from the converging squads. He replied with a couple of bursts from his own weapon, then fell on his stomach behind a rock and commenced reloading.

Perhaps it was because their experience had prejudiced them against all forces of law; perhaps it was merely sympathy with the underdog that impelled Sally and Marlin to pull mentally for the fugitive.

"That's no protection!" breathed Sally. They'll have him between a crossfire. Why doesn't he make a dash for it?"

"Where'll he dash?" queried Marlin.

For answer, Sally opened the door a crack and called sharply, "Here!"

The outlaw glanced desperately over his shoulder, then, crouching and dodging, he made a zigzag retreat up the hill. A rattle of shots accompanied this daring retreat. It was incredible that such an open target could escape the murderous bullets coming from all directions.

A final spurt and the fugitive fell sprawling across the threshold. Marlin dragged him inside as Sally slammed and bolted the door. Blood spurted from a neck wound and the outlaw clutched at his side, groaning.

"Done for—Thanks!" he gasped. "You better—" The effort at speech ended in a gasp.

The sound of running boots on the gravel, followed by a peremptory knock, indicated the arrival of the posse.

"Open up! This is the law!" an imperative voice called.

Sally tugged at the wounded man.

"Stall 'em off!" she whispered tensely. "I'll get him back inside."

With a hopeless gesture, Marlin tried to restrain her. "We'll only get ourselves in dutch—We can't hope to—"

Her look of scorn checked the protest. Shrugging, he lifted the desperately wounded man and supported him into the tunnel. Once erect, the outlaw seemed able to stumble along by leaning heavily on the bare-footed girl. Marlin closed the door and gave attention to the increasing demands from out in front.

He unlatched the swinging window.

"What's up?" he demanded.

A stocky figure detached itself from the group of twelve or fifteen bunched around the door.

"You're obstructing the law! Open that door!"

"Easy now," returned Marlin. "I'm not obstructing any law—I just want to know what it's all about? Who are you?"

"Sheriff Bates of Grinnell County. You're harboring an outlaw—the Picaroon Kid."

"Never heard of him. What'd he do?"

"Held up a band, for one thing," snapped the sheriff. "Wanted for other jobs and for killing two deputies. You gonna open that door?"

"Sure, I'll open it," Marlin spoke slowly, trying to give Sally time. "The poor devil's carcass is full of lead—no danger of his getting away."

Withdrawing, Marlin methodically fastened the window, then had an ostentatiously difficult time manipulating the door lock.

"Cut out that stalling!" called the sheriff furiously. "Are you gonna open up, or do we smash our way in?"

Marlin opened the door. With an impatient grunt, the sheriff brushed past him, glaring around uncertainly.

"Where'd you hide him?"

The outlaw's gun lay on the floor where it had been dropped in his fall, and a trail of blood led across the board floor. The sheriff snatched up the weapon, then crossed the room in a stride, flinging open the inner door. He peered down the tunnel.

"Some hideout!" he commented. "We'll look into this. Come on, men."

Marlin moved ahead of them, managing to delay progress by feeling his way with extreme caution through the dark passage. Eventually, they emerged on the shelving ledge.

"Where'd he go?" demanded the sheriff, surveying the scene.

"You know as much as I do."

A hasty search of bunkhouses and cook shack was sufficient to show that they were unoccupied. Two or three of the posse discovered a continuation of the blood trail, and they followed it to the descent which led to the sphere. Marlin's anxious eyes caught a glimpse of a bare foot disappearing in the entrance pipe. No one else was in sight.

"What's that big ball?" demanded the sheriff, staring.

"You've got me."

The blood trail led unmistakably toward the sphere. Soon the sheriff was peering curiously through the opening.

"The Kid's inside all right. Blood smears all down the pipe. Somebody climb in after him."

The men looked uncertainly at one another. It would be a simple matter for any armed person inside to put a bullet through the first head that showed itself. The sheriff evidently had no relish for the prospect and did not care to designate anyone for the job. He turned to Marlin.

"You go in there," he ordered.

"Tell your buddies they'll save trouble by bein' reasonable. Tell 'em to pass the Kid out. If they don't we'll toss a few tear gas bombs inside. You gonna do it?"

"What else can I do?"

With some forcible assistance from behind, Marlin worked his way down the tube. At the inner edge, hands grasped him by the shoulders and helped him to land on a floor of some kind.

"You tell 'em what I said!" came the sheriff's voice. "No stalling!"

His eyes unaccustomed to the darkness, Marlin allowed himself to be guided along some sort of a wooden platform. It slanted at an angle which made walking difficult. The guiding hands proved to be DuChane's.

"This is a hell of a mess," the latter breathed. "What's to be done?"

"Give up the outlaw. We're trapped in here like rats," Marlin answered. "If we don't come through, they'll toss in tear bombs. Can any of you imagine what that would be like in this place?"

"Leave it to that fool Sally!" McGruder said harshly.

The girl turned on him with a spiteful retort as an impatient call reached them from outside. Marlin raised his voice.

"Give me a chance!" he bellowed. The words echoed through the hollow interior. "It's dark in here. I've got to find 'em, haven't I?" He dropped his voice to a whisper. "How's the wounded jasper?"

"Passed out," DuChane informed him. "I'll lead you to him."

Feeling their way, they emerged in a box-like enclosure partly filled with tools. Maw Barstow, holding a feeble flashlight, squatted beside a huddled mass, which was evidently the wounded man. Cradling his head in her lap was Pearl. An accidental shifting of the flashlight beam revealed her tranquil, Madonna-like smile as she gazed down at the blood-smeared face.

"Sorry," Marlin announced. "We've got to get rid of this bad bozo. How's he doing?"

"You ain't gonna move the pore critter!" countered Maw fiercely.

Protest was futile. DuChane settled the argument by seizing the shrieking woman and holding her while Marlin gathered up the unconscious outlaw and felt his way back toward the opening. He was nearly thrown from his feet once as the platform—apparently the whole sphere—gave an unexpected lurch.

"Where's the place?" he demanded, sensing figures in the darkness surrounding. "I can't see the light."

Sally's laugh reached him shrilly.

"And what's more, you won't."

He paused, uncomprehending. Link's squeaky voice brought the explanation.

"They can't get us now. McGruder and me levered the pipe out with a board. You oughta see the stuff pour in."

The full enormity of this was slow in penetrating Marlin's mind.

"What's that!" called DuChane, his voice rising in alarm. He came stumbling toward them in the darkness. "Now isn't that fine! It isn't enough that we're trapped in here, but we've got to make the trap foolproof by blocking the only way out!"

Unmindful of the stormy exchange of insults and recriminations that surged around him, Marlin picked his way back to the tool room and deposited his groaning charge at Maw Barstow's feet.

"Better dress the wounds," he commented. "Where's Eli?"

"Somewhere down there," Maw replied vaguely. "Pearlie, darlin', help me get this bloody shirt offen the pore dear."

CHAPTER SIX

Returning to the others, Marlin found DuChane holding forth in a profane diatribe, which included not only McGruder, Link, and Sally, but all their antecedents.

"There's nothing to get excited over," Marlin interposed, calmly. "What difference does it make?"

"Difference?" DuChane roared. "Has it occurred to you that we've no possible way to get out of here? That ooze must have filled up the opening solidly by now."

"But the pipe is still projecting from the outside. Our sheriff friend will probably have gumption enough to force it in, just as we did. He'll be plenty mad by the time he finishes the job, but as far as I can see this merely delays our coming-out party for a few hours."

"And makes it tougher," growled DuChane. Marlin's words, nevertheless, seemed to have a quieting effect on his anger. His mood changed.

"We're in for it, but they can't pin anything on me. I served the rap for my little accident with a gun. Slinky here is likely to go up for a stretch, just on general principles. McGruder—now that baby has a bad conscience or he wouldn't have been so anxious to close the entrance. It wouldn't surprise me if—"

"Mind your own business!" snarled the detective. "Loud-mouthed blabbers like you is like to wake up with a knife in their ribs."

"So! A killer! One of the breed that sticks a knife in your back! What say, Dave—shall I teach him a lesson?"

There was a scuffle in the dark. "You lemme go!" roared McGruder. "I'll—" The words ended in a jolting gasp as two bodies struck the floor.

The thrashing limbs and bodies flailed for a moment, eliciting a wholehearted round of abuse from Sally as they almost knocked her feet from under. After a minute, DuChane arose.

"No weapons," he reported. "Bad boys shouldn't make threats unless they've got something to back 'em up with. Next time," he added ominously, "I'll cave your teeth in."

There was a faintly muttered response as McGruder retired to a safer distance.

"Where's Eli?" again demanded Marlin.

"He left us here," DuChane replied, "saying he was going down to the control room. Wonder if he has any way of lighting this—Oh, hello!"

A sudden radiance engulfed them.

Blinking, they stared at each other—at their surroundings.

The tilted surface on which they stood was apparently nothing more than scaffolding in the unfinished portion of the sphere. The boxes and crates they had loaded were distributed around the closed entrance hole. Peering upward, they looked into a network of girders, bracing the huge expanse, weirdly lighted here and there with single bulbs—evidently a temporary lighting arrangement for the workmen.

Below the level of their vision, also on a slant, was a partly enclosed portion of three or four levels, resembling a ship's superstructure. The humming noise of a dynamo accompanied the establishment of light service. Thornboldt emerged from a doorway and stood with head tilted back, surveying the bleak interior.

"Close the opening," he called out, catching sight of the group on the platform.

An involuntary laugh greeted the order.

Annoyed at the failure of his command to produce activity, the scientist worked his way up to the platform, emerging between the endshafts of a ladder. At the point in the hull where the pipe had penetrated, a bulging mass of the lava-like substance was slowly hardening.

He grunted. "Temporarily that will do. Later it must be covered with metal."

DuChane winked at Sally. "Anchors aweigh!" he sang. "Heave ho and a bottle of rum! Stand by for the good ship Thornboldt. But look ere, Eli, what about the eight?"

"Eh?"

"Seems to me Pearl predicted we'd make our start when there were four men, four gals, beside yourself. According to my reckoning, it doesn't count out."

"You ask me to take stock in such superstition? Am I a scientist or a Hottentot?"

Another lurch caused them all to grasp at near objects for support.

"What makes it do that?" demanded Sally, nervously. "Ever since we climbed in it's been acting like a horse with the heaves."

"It's the sphere turning and settling," DuChane informed her. His arm encircled her waist and she struggled—though not too violently, Marlin thought—to break away. Notice the floor's tilting? Won't be long before it stands straight up."

"Four and four," muttered the Dane into his beard. "There should be eight instead of seven. Where is that girl?"

Catching a glimpse of Pearl in the tool enclosure, he strode toward it.

"Oh no—he isn't superstitious!" commented DuChane.

"If we could rig up a periscope—push it through the soft part inside of the pipe—we might stand a chance of observing what goes on outside," Marlin suggested.

Without enthusiasm, DuChane agreed that it was a good idea. Releasing his hold on Sally, he followed Marlin down the ladder and they began an investigation of the more nearly finished section of the interior.

Some of the machinery they found understandable, much of it was strange. All loose objects had been tumbled into corners—probably had rolled around the circumference of whatever confined space they happened to be in, as the sphere slowly accomplished its rotation. But the supplies for the most part had been packed in anticipation of severe jolts. There was a really enormous supply of canned goods and other food items in sealed containers, but as yet no bunks had been erected in the doorless staterooms.

In one compartment they found a disarray of packing cases heaped together along one sidewall. One box had been crushed, revealing a gleaming cylinder.

"What are you doing there?" demanded Thornboldt from the doorway.

"If these happen to be instruments, perhaps you can tell us if there's a periscope in the lot," returned DuChane.

Eli fell to examining the boxes. "Try this one," he suggested. "Yes, that's a good idea. Very good." He hurried away, leaving them wondering at his unusual good spirits.

The instrument they unearthed was all that could be desired. "I believe," Marlin commented, "we can get this through by encasing it in a protective sheath."

"How'll we get the sheath off?"

"It can be done. We need a tube large enough to admit passage of the instrument. It can be just a rolled strip of sheet iron. We'll streamline it by welding the end to a point. When we've worked it through the mass far enough to project beyond the large pipe, we'll slide in the periscope. Last of all, we take a good solid rod, attach it to the rear projection of our sheath, and shove. When the sheath has cleared the top, it'll drop off, leaving the periscope head exposed."

"Might work," DuChane acknowledged. "You've an ingenious mind. But we'd better wait until dark. Less chance of being observed by the august forces of law and order."

"It'll be well along in the night before we've finished," returned Marlin. He caught hold of a doorpost as the sphere gave another shuddering lurch.

In their quest for material, they came upon Eli in the lower level of the superstructure. He was making adjustments throughout a bank of coils, which seemed to constitute the major element of his apparatus. Pausing curiously, DuChane demanded:

"What's that for?"

Eli grunted, but the pride of an inventor won out over disdain.

"You could not understand," he informed them ungraciously. "Locked in these coils is a power that will make the name of Elias Thornboldt outstanding in history. A magnetic field in which occurs such a stress as the atom has never known causes polarization of the repulsion plates below this floor which is—how can I express it—the opposite of magnetism, of attraction of the force of gravity."

"In other words," retorted DuChane, "anti-gravity." He nudged Marlin. "Professor Lamberton says your conclusions are unsound—that it would be impossible to build up a sufficiently strong magnetic field to accomplish the results you claim."

"That nincompoop!" exploded the scientist. "That stuffed piece of shirt! What does he know about atomic stress? Nothing! Yet he presumes—" Eli paused suspiciously. "Who told you about Lamberton?"

"Oh, we get around!"

The bearded scientist snorted. "Why bandy words? To show up Lamberton in all his stupidity, I have only to do this—"

With a dramatic gesture, he thrust home the prongs of a huge switch that occupied the central panel of a control board in front of the coil. Involuntarily, Marlin braced himself for a shock. Nothing happened. Nothing, at least, beyond a faint hum which emanated from the towering apparatus.

"Well?" queried DuChane impudently.

Eli shook his beard impatiently. "What did you expect? First it is necessary to build up a magnetic potential. Then, with this lever, I release the current through the repulsion plates." He caressed the device but refrained from demonstrating. "Naturally, I will make the first tests with utmost caution. The lever acts as a rheostat, by which the power is applied in any degree required, governing the acceleration. If I should move it to the extreme limit we would be hurled away from the earth with such violence as to crush every bone."

"How about steering?" queried Marlin. "Wouldn't you be condemned to travel in a straight line from any object which the plates happened to be facing at the start?"

"Do you take me for a numskull? Naturally the plates are segmented. They can be turned like a—like a—"

"Like the sections of a venetian blind," interposed DuChane. "I get you. And—er—when do you start?"

Eli frowned. "I shall not delay long. All essentials are in place—the storage batteries, fully charged to furnish current for at least seven months, the dynamos, the conversion coils. First comes the trial flight. It will be brief—but sufficient to astonish the world. Then, when I have enjoyed the sight of Lamberton and those imbecile financiers groveling in the dust, I shall finish the sphere—without their assistance—and go—who knows where? To the moon, the planets—"

His grandiloquent vision was interrupted by another of the periodic lurches, which caused them all to grasp for support. Overhead, the girders groaned as they accommodated themselves to a new stress. Somewhere, a heavy object fell.

DuChane suddenly doubled up with mirth.

"Look!" he chortled. "Oh, this is good!"

Marlin followed the direction of his pointing finger. Involuntarily, he smiled.

"By rights," he commented grimly, "our bones ought to be crushed to powder. Well, that settles that."

Thornboldt stared blankly at the rheostat lever. His body, flung against it by the upheaval of the sphere, had pushed it to the extreme limit, which he had warned would produce dire results.

"It means nothing!" he protested hollowly. "One faulty connection could make the whole thing a failure. Besides, how can you expect a lifting power that was intended for a hollow sphere to lift hundreds of tons of mud? Leave me alone. How can I work with such imbecile interruptions?"

They withdrew, leaving him staring with frowning contemplation at the ineffective starting lever.

"The old coot had me wondering at that," Marlin confided, as he and DuChane set about their task of installing the periscope. "I'm glad to have it settled."

They worked steadily into the night, pausing only to take part in a meal concocted from the ship's stores.

The outlaw had been made as comfortable as possible in one of the doorless staterooms, but was tossing in semi-delirium. He had been struck by at least six bullets, as reported by Sally. "Hmm!" grunted Marlin, busy with his welding torch. "Not much chance of his pulling through."

"Pearl says he will," returned Sally. She spoke with an air of amusement—almost of mystery. "Know what that girl had us do? She insisted on our puncturing the blister over that opening in the shell and drawing off about a quart of that gummy stuff for poultices. Since the idea came from Pearl, Maw thinks it must be the berries."

"Sounds unsanitary, to say the least."

"Oh, I don't know," DuChane disagreed. "Certain clays are used medicinally for drawing out inflammation. Come to think of it, this stuff resembles antiphlogistin as much as anything."

"If it works," observed Marlin, "we might put the goo on the market and make our fortunes."

The others had all turned in when Marlin and DuChane finished their task. As nearly as they could judge, the panoramic sight would be a success, although little could be discerned through it in the darkness except the outline which separated the blackness below the crater rim from the somewhat brighter hue of the sky.

"Frankly, now that we've accomplished the job, I don't know what good it's going to do," DuChane grumbled, as they turned to seek out their sleeping pallets. "If the sheriff starts to dig his way in, or if he chooses to do it just for meanness—he can snap the head off in a second."

Marlin grunted. The same thought had occurred to him, but he had kept it to himself. It had seemed better for the morale of the group to offer a show of activity.

As it was, their example had inspired even McGruder and Link to chip in toward opening packing cases, distributing the bedding, and otherwise providing temporary living quarters. All were sufficiently tired to sleep. Marlin dropped off almost instantly from exhaustion when he rolled himself in his blankets.

CHAPTER SEVEN

He woke with a stifling sense of oppression. In that indefinite period between sleeping and waking, he struggled with a terrified conviction that the whole mass of the enclosing sphere was caving in on him, smothering, crushing his chest, grinding him against the floor. For some minutes, he seemed unable to move. Eventually, his head clearing somewhat, he struggled up, gasping for breath and fighting a surge of nausea. The crushing sensation had been so vivid that it was several minutes before he could overcome it.

From an adjoining cubicle, the moans of the wounded outlaw penetrated his consciousness. He rose painfully, mindful of sore and stiffened muscles, and stumbled out onto the ramp.

Overhead, the scattered lights which gave a faint illumination to the network of girders, were casting weird, swaying shadows, as they did after every lurch of the sphere.

It was such a lurch, Marlin realized, that probably woke him. The floor, he noticed, had returned more nearly to level.

Maw Barstow had spread her pallet across the bare opening of the outlaw's room, and lay there like a watchdog—anything but a lovely sight with her upturned face and open mouth. She was making hard work of sleep and did not stir when Marlin stepped over her and knelt beside the suffering figure inside.

A rag was immersed in a pan of water at the side of the pallet. Surmising its purpose, he squeezed a little between the feverish lips and then wiped off the drawn face. The muddy stuff of the poultice had oozed out around the neck wound. Marlin wiped some of it away and adjusted the bandage, then pulled down the cover to see if other bandages needed similar attention.

The outlaw, though wiry, seemed to have a rather frail physique. His face was smooth and boylike, almost sensitive, despite the hard set of the mouth. A tight bandage swathed the chest, but as Marlin's fingers felt along its edge he was struck by the soft, pliable texture of the flesh beneath.

For a minute, he paused, considering the faintly moaning figure. For some strange reason, chills raced up his spine.

Deliberately, he drew down the cover, until he could view the outstretched body. Then, very carefully, he restored the blanket to its place, tucking it carefully around the sleeping figure. The figure that was not a man—but a girl…

When he rose to leave a moment later, Pearl was framed in the doorway, her lips parted in the enigmatic smile, which belied the innocent vacuity of her eyes.

Marlin stepped over Maw Barstow's sleeping body and took the white-gowned girl gently by the arm.

"Better get back to your covers," he advised; then, softly: "Girl, oh girl! Maybe you've got something after all!"

When Marlin next awakened, it was to the rude shock of rough hands shaking him excitedly. He struggled up, his first impulse to strike out in resentment. It was DuChane.

"Wake up, Dave! For God's sake, wake up! I've got something to show you!"

Still half asleep, Marlin followed the other toward the ladder, which led to the scaffold by which they had first entered. He felt strangely lightheaded, nauseated, wobbly on his feet, and his muscles ached. Unsteadily, he followed the other up to the scaffold.

DuChane applied his eye to the periscope, then gestured.

"Look!" His voice was scarcely more than a whisper.

Marlin crouched before the eyepiece. He peered through it with vague bewilderment at first, then with growing interest—concern—amazement.

He spoke at last. His voice strained and unfamiliar.

"There's nothing out there! No ground—no hillside—no crater—no scaffolding—nothing! Nothing but stars. Stars and blackness."

DuChane moistened his lips.

"It's an illusion," whispered Marlin. "We can't be—"

He glanced up at the girders. The shadows were still shifting in a weird dance to the cadence of swaying lights.

"I know when it happened," he breathed hoarsely. "I woke up—a little past midnight—with a terrible sense of oppression. Felt as if I was being crushed. It must have been the acceleration."

DuChane swallowed. "Nothing like that now. In fact, it's just the opposite—a touch of weightlessness. We'd better find Eli—have it out with him."

The bearded scientist was snoring furiously on his pallet in the control room. They woke him without ceremony.

DuChane interrupted the diatribe that trembled on the older man's lips.

"What right had you to do this?" he accused. "How do you know you can get us back safely? Damn it all!" DuChane's anger rose as the full enormity of the situation broke over him. "How do you expect to steer the crazy thing—find your way back—land it? That dinky periscope is about as useful for guidance as a cigarette lighter in a blizzard!"

Eli stiffened. "If you gentlemen will kindly explain what you are talking about!"

"Why, you—!" DuChane broke off. "Mean to tell us you don't know?"

The scientist's blank stare continued.

"We're in space," Marlin informed him tersely.

The older man seemed unable to comprehend. A momentary triumph lighted in his eyes, then faded into suspicion.

"Go away!" he ordered gruffly. "I have no mood for silly jokes."

Still, he submitted as they assisted him to his feet and hustled him toward the periscope.

A few moments later, racing back to the control room, he began a feverish examination of instruments and dials.

"I understand now. Yes—it is clear. I should have known, but in dealing with new forces—one lacks the guidance of experience. Lamberton—that imbecile? How I shall laugh. Charlatan eh! Yes, yes. It was necessary to build up a sufficient potential—to do that naturally took a great deal longer—"

"Look here," interrupted DuChane. "Isn't it possible that the coating on the sphere somehow acted as a storage reservoir into which your current poured until it built up this—this terrific potential you've mentioned? I mean—well, perhaps this storing up of power multiplied the current generated by your dynamos, until they overcame the objection Lamberton pointed out—that of obtaining sufficient power to produce the atomic stress."

"Nonsense!" Eli retorted reddening. "That imbecile has not the brains to grasp even my basic theory. There is no connection between my conversion coils and the mud coating!"

"You have a ground of some sort, haven't you?"

"Certainly. The steel shell of the sphere—" The inventor paused abruptly. "That dense outer coating of clay—Yes, yes. It might so act." He paused in exasperation. "Gentlemen! Please kindly go away! Is it not enough that I have great responsibilities, but you must come around with your childish theorizing?"

By this time, the others had been awakened by the commotion, and were crowding around the control room entrance.

"Wha—what's up?" demanded Link.

Marlin looked at DuChane; DuChane returned the look.

"Somebody has to break the news," said Marlin grimly. His eyes swept the gathering. "You may as well have it straight. We're no longer on earth; we're in space."

"Whadda you mean—space?" Link was bewildered.

"This is a space vessel isn't it—built to rise from the earth and fly off into the void? Well, contrary to expectations, it's doing just that. How far above earth we are, there's no way of telling—but I'm inclined to think it's one hell of a long way."

CHAPTER EIGHT

In an ordinary group, such an announcement might have brought hysterical outbursts from the women and at least some kind of clamor from the men. Eli's motley guests were either slower of comprehension or else hardened to vicissitudes. McGruder turned a rather ghastly color, murmured, "Jees!" and sat down heavily on a packing box. No one else evinced more than bewilderment.

"So what?" queried Sally Camino. "Where are we going and how do we get back? Whose bright idea was this anyway?"

"Nobody's," Marlin informed her. "Eli left the force field in operation and accidentally pushed the starting lever last night. Since nothing happened, it never occurred to him to swing it back. The explanation seems to be that when enough power had accumulated, the anti-gravity polarization occurred, and we parted company with Mother Earth."

Link greeted this with a snicker. "I was just thinkin'," he explained when the others focused puzzled eyes upon him, "what a su'prise that sheriff an' his dep'ties is gonna have when they find the old mud-ball gone this mornin'. Maybe some of 'em was on guard when it whooshed up into the sky afore their eyes."

No one laughed.

"No use kidding ourselves," Marlin commented. "We're in a tough predicament. We don't know where the sphere is headed; there's nothing but that hopelessly inadequate periscope to guide it by, and personally, I don't see the ghost of a chance of our landing anywhere. We're just a mote of dust in the void of space."

"It's just like Pearlie said, ain't it dearie?" cackled Maw Barstow unexpectedly. "We are all goin' on a long journey. Pearlie never makes a mistake."

"Oh, I don't know!" retorted DuChane, slyly. "I could cite an instance. Or maybe it's just faulty arithmetic. There were to be four and four, not three and five—at least 'that's the way I heard it.'"

"And that's all you know, smarty," chuckled Maw.

Sally winked at the older woman, while Marlin controlled his features with an effort.

"Ask her when we're gonna land—and where at?" suggested Link, peering hopefully.

"Pearlie will tell us everything in her own good time," retorted Maw, grandly. "Won't you darlin'? Don't you want to tell us where we're goin'?"

The girl smiled sweetly, and uttered the first words Marlin had heard from her lips.

"There are so many stones."

McGruder laughed hoarsely. Maw checked him with a ferocious look. "Go on, dearie," she urged. "Tell us more?"

The girl stared upward, as if visioning something in the distance. Her words slurred together; she seemed only half-aware of speaking them.

"The world is a stone. There are many stones. So many lonely stones."

Marlin again experienced the uncanny sense of chills spiraling up his back—for no reason that he could comprehend. He looked uncertainly from one face to another. All were staring at the Sybil of the strange voyage.

Maw spoke with vague conviction. "That means something, and don't you mistake it. We'll have to figger it out. Pearlie don't always talk in plain words fer just ever'body to understand."

From behind the huge bank of coils, Elias Thornboldt emerged. He glowered in annoyance.

"Go away!" he ordered. "None of you are permitted in this room." He looked them over with sudden awareness and spoke bitterly. "What a crew for the pioneer flight into space! Instead of a distinguished gathering of world-famous scientists and statesmen, what do I have? Criminals! Go! Out of my sight!"

As they straggled out, DuChane observed with a show of resentment: "We might remind him that if it wasn't for a device rigged up by some of his despised crew, he wouldn't even know his contraption was off the ground."

Burning questions raced through Marlin's mind, but he frankly doubted the scientist's ability to answer them. A genius in his line Thornboldt might be; nevertheless, he was singularly impractical in other directions. One of Marlin's questions related to the persistence of almost normal gravity within the sphere. The explanation, DuChane suggested, must lie in the repulsion plates. While one surface exercised this force, the opposite surface compensated for it by exercising attraction. Though he tentatively accepted this theory for want of a better, Marlin was dissatisfied with it.

Another question related to the direction of their flight. Were they speeding toward or away from the sun? Was there danger of crashing into some planet, moon, or meteoric body, and if so could they avoid such a fate? Observations through the periscope might presently solve the question of direction. Possibly Eli had instruments which would help.

The days that followed settled down to a dull, monotonous routine. There was nothing—almost literally nothing—to do but eat, sleep, and chafe at the helplessness of their position.

Lacking any measurement of time in the uniform semi-gloom of the sphere, they established an arbitrary day of twenty-four hours. They slept and ate in accustomed routine and kept track of the days of the week.

The initial feeling that something must be done—and done immediately—toward getting out of the predicament, gradually gave way to a sense of hopeless resignation. When they goaded Eli with the necessity for action, he flew into violent rages. They realized at length that he was as much at a loss as any of the party.

How could they guide their course, when the limited observations possible through the periscope scarcely told them whether they were traveling toward the sun or away from it? They might, indeed, be hanging inert in space. Marlin contended that they were moving away from the sun.

"It's a cinch we started in that direction, since our ascent took place at night, when the sun was on the opposite side of the earth."

"If that's correct," growled DuChane, "it means that instead of roasting to death, we're doomed to perish of cold, when this hunk of dough gets so far away that there aren't any more of the sun's rays for it to absorb."

"We'll be dead of starvation long before that," Marlin added moodily.

The store of provisions seemed enormous at first glance. Now, faced by stern questions of survival, they calculated that it would actually last them not more than five months, and a careful rationing was instituted.

The water tanks would supply them for a period somewhat longer. Bathing and washing were restricted but not altogether denied, for the equipment included an efficient settling tank as well as an electric incinerator and an air-purifying system that was a credit to Eli's foresight.

"Evidently we'll starve to death before we have a chance to perish of thirst," was DuChane's comforting observation. "Unless the goo of our outside shell proves to be edible. It seems to have about every other property we could ask. Storage battery, heat absorber and distributor, healing agent, and waste converter."

He referred to their discovery that the waste products discharged through locks were seemingly absorbed by the clay-like outer coating. "I believe it digests the stuff.

Remember how the pit absorbed those birds and small animals that became imbedded in it?" reminded DuChane. "I sometimes feel as if—"

"As if what?" demanded Marlin, looking at him curiously.

"Nothing. I couldn't put it into words if I tried."

CHAPTER NINE

Curiosity centered for a while upon the outlaw, who was making a slow recovery. She—for after a few days her sex had become general knowledge—kept moodily to herself, having little to do with the other women and regarding the men with suspicion.

She gave her real name as Norma Hegstrom. DuChane, by persistent questioning, elicited the additional fact that she had escaped from some institution—possibly a school of correction—and adopted her masquerade on coming West in order to elude the search.

"The way I've got it figured out," he confided to Sally and Marlin, as they sat listlessly on the platform under the periscope, "in order to make good in her boy's disguise and to offset her underlying feminine appearance, she had to act tougher than any of the roughnecks she was thrown with. So, by degrees, she was drawn into the career of an outlaw.

"You'd almost think," he added reflectively, "that Earth spewed out this gang because we're a bunch of what the sociologists call unassimilable elements."

"What do you mean by that?" snapped Sally.

"With all respect to those present I suppose we could be spared about as well as any you could mention. Nobody here seems to have any home ties. There's no one back on Earth whose life will be affected by our departure. We haven't contributed anything constructive to society—in fact, on the average, we've been just general nuisances."

Marlin looked at him curiously. "You're implying—"

"I'm not implying a thing," DuChane evaded. He twisted around and picked up a jagged disc of metal. "We've got more serious problems to face. Recognize this?"

"It's the piece Slinky cut out of the opening with the blowtorch."

"Ever look at it?"

Marlin studied the other's face under the swinging shadows. Then he took the metal disc and peered at it closely.

Sally glanced from one serious face to the other. "Well," she demanded, "what's it all about?"

Without a word, Marlin passed her the fragment.

"Link said the blowtorch cut through it like butter," DuChane remarked grimly. "We've noticed how the clay covering digests waste material—tin cans included."

Sally turned the piece over curiously, ran her fingers over the serrated surface, held it up to the light.

"So that's all there is between us and—" She hesitated. "Why it's half eaten through in places—like something rusted. Is it my imagination, or can you see through it?"

"Imagination," assured Marlin. He took the fragment and held it before his eyes. "No, by thunder! A couple of pinpoint holes have been eaten clear through it."

After a moment, Sally slowly rose.

"No use saying anything to the others," Marlin suggested, noting the listless drag of her bare feet as she started toward the ladder.

She glanced over her shoulder disdainfully.

"What do you take me for?"

But the secret was not long in becoming general property. Len McGruder, who seemed to prefer devious and furtive ways of accomplishing even obvious things, must have been listening from one of many possible hiding places, or at least observing from a distance, for he produced the steel fragment at the next mealtime gathering.

"What's this about the old ball goin' to pieces?" he demanded. "What're you tryin' to put over?"

Marlin eyed him with distaste. "As far as you are concerned," he said slowly, "nothing. There's only one reason why I denied myself the pleasure of letting you know the fate in store for you—and that's because I knew you were so yellow you'd spill it and frighten the rest."

"Yellow, eh!" McGruder jumped to his feet in a rage. He appealed to the group. "What do you think of this bird—and a couple of others I could mention—" he glanced meaningly at DuChane and Sally—"gettin' their heads together to figger out a way of savin' theirselves while the rest of us is left to rot in this stinkin' blob of mud? How's that for yellow?"

DuChane laughed mirthlessly.

"If there's any comfort in the knowledge," he said, "there'll be no escape for any of us. The mud coating has a faculty of digesting every inert substance it contacts. Very convenient for taking care of our waste products—but unfortunate because it applies also to our habitation."

"You mean it's gonna eat through the shell?" demanded Link, his weasel eyes glittering.

Marlin shrugged.

"But we gotta do something! Does Eli know?"

The slinky one peered around the table, finding no reassurance in any of the blank faces. He gulped and subsided.

Later, he and McGruder constituted themselves a delegation to lay the problem before the scientist. Eli had practically barricaded himself in the control room. At his bellowed command meals were brought to him at irregular intervals by Maw Barstow. He rarely appeared outside of his retreat, except when he ventured forth briefly for a peep through the periscope.

"What'd he say?" demanded DuChane, when the two returned from their self-imposed mission.

"None o' your business!" McGruder snarled.

"The old coot don't seem to get it," complained Link. "All he done was to rant about how they gypped him when they sold him the steel."

The pale-featured outlaw girl, Norma, taking a listless turn along the ramp in a robe provided from Maw Barstow's meager store, was an inadvertent listener to this exchange. She seemed inclined to brush by, but suddenly her deep-set eyes glowed with fire.

"It's a joke!" she contributed unexpectedly. "You save me from the law, doctor up my carcass—and for what?"

"Does seem rather futile," agreed Marlin, sympathetically. He reflected that as her hair grew longer she was becoming a great deal more feminine in appearance. The wound in her neck was by now little more than a scar.

Under his scrutiny, her lips tightened and she abruptly walked away.

DuChane's eyes followed until she disappeared behind the curtain which served as a doorway for her sleeping compartment.

"Y'know," he volunteered, "there's something about that kid I could almost tumble for."

"Cut it out!" was Marlin's sharp response.

"What do you mean?"

Marlin did not answer. He was, in fact, puzzled to know why he had spoken.

"I'll tell you what you mean!" DuChane said heatedly. "You've got your eyes on this dame, same as you've had 'em on Sally. Anything that looks like competition gets your nanny. Well, Marlin I'm serving notice that where women are concerned I do my own picking. The other man's claim-stakes mean nothing to me."

"That's the talk!" approved McGruder. "What the hell! There's enough to go around, not countin' old Eli, and we don't know what's gonna happen tomorrow. I got my eye on that little—"

"Shut up!" blazed Marlin.

He eyed the ex-detective with burning distaste.

He could have reminded them that he was in a position to enforce his edicts, being in possession of the only weapon. They knew this, however, and it was already a source of mounting antagonism.

What had caused him to bristle at signs of interest toward the feminine portion of the party? It wasn't that he wanted any of them for himself, though he sensed a challenge in Sally's eyes and acknowledged that she was desirable in her way. Norma, too, gave promise of becoming attractive as she regained her vitality. But his attitude was inspired by something deeper.

Perhaps it was an instinctive prescience that man-woman rivalry would inevitably bring trouble. This and a very special feeling that Pearl must be protected in her childlike innocence. The covetous looks with which McGruder regarded her were unmistakable. The very thought of them rankled in Marlin like a sacrilege. Maw Barstow was an efficient watchdog, but the shady detective would stop at nothing he thought he could get away with.

From this time, DuChane mockingly defied Marlin's half-expressed edict, by ostentatiously "making a play" for both Sally and Norma. His eyes taunted Marlin to do something about it. And Marlin, knowing that he had no reasonable excuse for interfering, could only chafe inwardly and pretend to have no interest in the matter.

The result was that he withdrew more and more into himself, holding aloof from the others, becoming increasingly morose and distant.

CHAPTER TEN

Seemingly least imaginative of them all, it was odd that Link should be the first to crack under the strain.

From the time of the disclosure that their hull was slowly corroding under the chemical action of the clay, he had appeared frightened and morose. Once or twice, as Marlin approached him on isolated portions of the superstructure, he slunk away in a peculiar manner. One day—for they still called their alternation of sleeping and waking periods a "day"—he failed to show up for meals.

When he did not appear the second day, the group aroused from its apathetic indifference sufficiently to institute a search.

He was crouching behind some packing boxes in the storeroom, and fled with wild shrieks on being discovered.

He managed to hide himself again, and the search was dropped. Some hours later they discovered him furtively clamoring among the girders overhead.

From this time on, the girders became his abode. His weasel face, nearly hidden by the long growth of hair, peered down at them from odd angles with alert suspicion. He resembled an unkempt monkey clad in tattered shirt and trousers. If they attempted to approach or tried to lure him down, he shrieked and chattered at them, and retreated to more precarious heights, until they desisted, fearful of making him fall.

"Hunger'll bring him down," DuChane said. And it did. During one of the sleep periods, he raided the storeroom and created such havoc that Maw Barstow formed a habit of leaving his ration of food and water on a box in plain sight.

When all were apparently asleep, he would stealthily slip down and snatch the food, wolfing it like a wild creature, ready to scamper for safety at the slightest noise.

Watching from concealment, Marlin saw him do this a couple of times, but made no effort to trap him.

And for Marlin, there were more important concerns. Isolated from the rest, he sat for hours at a time before the periscope, trying to arrive at some theory regarding their position in space.

One thing was established by now. The sphere had developed a lazy rotation of its own, presenting its two hemispheres alternately to the sun and giving the surface on which the periscope projected a "day" of about five hours.

Even without visual observation, the shifting heat areas within the globe would have led to the same conclusion. The clay-like coating seemed to have the property of diffusing the sun's rays throughout its mass. Possibly it would have been burned to a crisp on one side without such rotation. The side that was receiving the direct rays radiated a gentle heat through the walls, and this area of radiation traveled slowly around the circumference.

To Marlin, this rotation seemed to deny the activity of the antigravity plates, yet the maintenance of gravity indicated that at least they retained some of their function. To account for this seeming paradox and others, he evolved a set of theories. Some he was able to verify.

From the first, he had found it difficult to swallow DuChane's surmise that gravity was maintained within the sphere through some mysterious reaction from the obverse surfaces of the repulsion plates. To satisfy his doubts, he wormed his way through a narrow opening between the hull and girders supporting the super-structure, until he reached the edge of a segmented bank of repulsion plates.

He found them heavily insulated on the upper side, as if to prevent the force from exerting its full strength in that direction. By lying in a cramped position, he was able to extend an arm through a narrow crevice and to touch the under side of the plates.

His exploring fingers contacted a fragment of some sort-a pebble or hardened lump of clay. Detaching it from the surface, he fingered it exploringly. When his fingers relaxed, the lump escaped and instantly snapped back to the plate, as if held by a taut rubber band. He recovered the fragment and tried the same thing experimentally, with the same result.

There was no mistake. Objects released below the anti-gravity plates dropped toward them, just as did objects released from above. If anything, the attraction of the underside was stronger. In point of fact, the supposed anti-gravity plates were gravity plates.

Convinced of something he had vaguely suspected, Marlin retired to his usual vantage point—the observation scaffold—to think matters out.

He was vaguely disturbed when Sally clambered up the ladder and joined him.

"You're up to something?" she accused. "Tell Sally what it's all about."

"I'd only bore you."

"What's the difference? I'm bored anyway."

She sat beside him on the edge of the platform, bare feet protruding from her threadbare slacks. Marlin was quite certain that she wouldn't resist if he put his arm around her, but he squelched any such impulse. Too many times he had seen DuChane's arm occupying that position.

"All right," he observed. "You asked for it." He told her what he had discovered.

"Well," she asked, "what of it?"

"This is the way I'd explain it. I think the criticism of Thornboldt's principle, advanced by orthodox scientists, was probably justified. Such an enormous application of energy would be needed to effect the stress required for anti-gravity polarization, that it was a practical impossibility. Yet somehow this enormous power was generated for the brief moment which marked the plunge of our vessel into outer space."

"I think we ought to christen the old ball," she remarked irrelevantly. "How about calling it what Bart suggested—the Thornboldt?"

"I suppose the inventor is entitled to some credit," Marlin agreed absently. "But to figure this out: Let's assume a generator or storage battery capable of delivering current of one ampere strength for a hundred hours. Suppose it should release the same amount of current within a single hour. The strength of the current would obviously be multiplied a hundred times, wouldn't it? Suppose the same current were released in a single minute. It would be multiplied six thousand times. Suppose it were released in a second, what would be its strength?"

"I'm no good at figures," replied Sally, fidgeting.

"Thirty-six thousand amperes!" Marlin told her impressively. "That's a lot of stepping up. Eli claims his batteries are capable of supplying current for several months, and while I don't know their capacity, it must be considerable. Suppose most of this potential current was drained off by the shell of our vessel, acting like a Leyden jar or accumulator, and then released in one titanic discharge. Don't you see? This must have accomplished the near-impossible—the polarization of the repulsion plates, resulting in the anti-gravity reaction."

"You sure deal out jawbreakers when you get started," Sally shrugged.

"All right," he went on imperturbably. "The intense discharge probably lasted only a moment—but that was sufficient. It shot our sphere away from the earth as if it had been fired from a cannon—sent it with an initial momentum which took us far beyond Earth's attraction and must still be continuing undiminished in the vacuum of space."

Sally yawned and rose. "What you need is a classroom," she said. "I'll pass the word along in case any of the rest feel the need of brushing up on their education."

Her departure scarcely disturbed Marlin's train of thought. His theory, of course, gave birth to other perplexing problems. How account for the fact that neither sphere nor passengers were crushed by the enormous acceleration?

He had an answer for that one. Logically, he reasoned, they owed their salvation to the fact that they, too, were subject to the momentary repulsion of the activated plates. Repulsion hurled them violently away—acceleration pressed them back. The two forces practically cancelled out. Possibly the insulation on the upper surfaces of the plates gave acceleration a slight edge, causing the crushing sensation Marlin had felt at the onset of their flight.

But the anti-gravity force was no longer in effect—probably had lasted not more than a few seconds. What had caused the plates to become imbued with an opposite force—an attractive force akin to gravity?

To answer this, Marlin found himself seeking analogies in the realm of electrical phenomena.

A magnet, he reflected, is a bar of iron in which the movements of the molecules are so organized as to keep the lines of their magnetic axis parallel—all the molecular north poles pointing toward the same end of the bar. It is accomplished by placing the bar in a larger magnetic field, and it is made permanent by tempering—which fixes the molecules in permanent alignment.

Thornboldt's atomic polarization principle must be similar. Under terrific stress, the molecules of the repulsion plates, and their constituent atoms, were polarized in such a way that they exercised the force of repulsion. But when the stress was released, there would be no tempering to maintain the molecular set. They would—in a manner of speaking—snap back, like rubber bands released from tension, not quite to their original condition, but to a condition tending toward the opposite of that occasioned by the stress.

The attractive property now inherent in the plates, in other words, was a reaction from the terrific stress of their momentary anti-gravity polarization.

It was notable that there had been no interruption of the electrical power which supplied current for cooking and waste incineration, operated the air-purifying apparatus and refrigeration plant, and kept their lighting system in force. Evidently, Marlin decided, the storage batteries—if they had been drained of their charges prior to the impulse, which hurled them into space—must have recovered, as batteries do when given a rest. He inclined also to the opinion that the sphere itself generated electricity through the expansion and contraction of the outer coating as it slowly revolved.

Sally appeared to avoid him after this encounter—or so Marlin imagined. He had a notion that she had been piqued by DuChane's pursuit of Norma, and wanted to show the man a thing or two by giving Marlin an opportunity to make love to her. His failure to rise to the bait had not endeared him to her.

He told himself that he did not care—but, in truth, he felt his isolation. It was comforting even to have Pearl creep up to the periscope ledge beside him, as she did at rare intervals. He fell into the habit of talking to her, as a relief from the close-mouthed silence that had grown upon him. It was better, at any rate, than talking to himself, and helped him to orient his ideas.

"Sometimes, Pearl," he confided, "I have a feeling that you sense what I'm trying to say better than I understand it myself. It's cockeyed—but a fellow develops queer fancies in a weird situation like this."

She smiled amiably.

"I even find myself assuming that you know what's behind all this. I suppose it's your air of calm assurance—or the lucky way you seemed to hit things back there on Earth. And here I go, with another screwy idea—that there is something behind it all."

He applied his eye to the periscope. It was on the night side, and only an impenetrable expanse of blackness, studded with bright, unblinking points of light, rewarded his gaze. Relaxing, he faced the girl.

"Reason tells me that we're the victims of a freakish accident. Yet I find myself assuming—"

He checked the sentence, glancing around self-consciously for possible eavesdroppers. With a dreamy expression Pearl was looking at—or beyond him.

"It's a comfort to talk to you," he confessed. "You make it easier to express the inexpressible. What was I saying? Oh, yes."

He frowned. "I get to fancying sometimes that the crew of us were brought together, herded into this incredible monstrosity, and then spewed forth in accordance with some age-old plan. It's almost as if the little world we're in had a life of its own and had been sent forth with the blessings of the parent Earth to work out its own destiny. What do you think, Pearl? In your infinite wisdom—or simplicity—tell me. At least it *could* be true."

The girl's lips parted. "It could be true," she echoed.

He shrugged. Often you could get a response from her by making an emphatic effort, but it was usually like this—some amiable repetition of the words you put in her mouth.

"All right," he retorted, as if she had contradicted him, "say that I'm screwy! But tell me—what do we know about other possible states of consciousness? We think we understand human consciousness—because we're experiencing it. We credit animals with consciousness because they act in a limited way like humans. But how do we know there aren't other phases of consciousness? How do we know that a tree isn't a conscious entity, or a rock, or this globe—or the Earth? How do we know?"

"How do we know?" parroted the girl. She smiled up at his tense features, as if trying to please him. Beyond her, in the shadowy obscurity of the girders, he caught a glimpse of Link's monkey-like face peering furtively down at them.

He broke off abruptly. "You're a bad influence, Pearl. You encourage a fellow to voice crazy ideas. First thing I know, I'll be swinging around on girders myself."

CHAPTER ELEVEN

McGRUDER, who as a rule evinced little interest in matters beyond eating, sleeping, and following the feminine members of the party with pig-like, calculating eyes, was the one who made the discovery.

He had climbed to the observation scaffold and peeped idly through the periscope. His yell of dismay reverberated through the interior of the vessel.

"We're gonna hit the moon!" he shouted, as the others scrambled into view.

Marlin gained the platform. "What's the idea!" he demanded sharply. "We aren't within a million miles of the moon."

McGruder gulped, gesturing toward the periscope.

Marlin remained glued to the instrument until DuChane cut in roughly: "Give someone else a chance. What's out there?"

Marlin relinquished his post. His voice sounded unnaturally strained. "See for yourself."

It did look like a shrunken version of the old familiar moon—a gleaming disc shining brilliantly against the inky blackness of space.

"We're approaching a solar body of some sort," Marlin told the others, who had struggled up to the platform. His eyes inadvertently sought Pearl. "Maybe this is the answer to—" He broke off.

DuChane straightened from the eyepiece.

"Two to one it means a crackup," he commented. "Unless Eli knows how to guide this shebang—and I don't believe he does."

Nevertheless, they reported the approaching crisis to the inventor. Eli had grown more eccentric as the voyage continued. His hair and beard were wilder; he talked incoherently.

When he had assured himself that they were actually approaching a stellar body, he displayed a great deal of energy, rushing from periscope to control room and back again; but they had no way of knowing the result of this activity, and received scant satisfaction from his impatient responses to questions.

"My private opinion," Marlin observed, later, "is that his instruments have no more control over this vessel than if we'd left them in that pit back on Earth. All connections must have burned out in that incredible burst of power that hurled us into space."

But at least, Eli made a great show of adjusting his switches and levers. Whether he planned to effect a landing or was trying to avoid the approaching body, was a secret locked in his own dome-like head.

In time this new menace became commonplace and life lapsed into its dull routine, with Marlin alone spending a great deal of time observing their progress toward the stellar body. On one occasion, Pearl paid him one of her infrequent visits.

He looked up as the girl climbed from the ladder.

"Better run along," he said abruptly. "It's considered bad medicine for you to chin with me."

SHE stopped beside him and cocked her head on one side, for all the world like a bird listening for a worm.

"It is so lonely," she said yearningly.

"You—lonely?" he repeated in surprise. "Didn't know you ever felt that way."

With a suggestion of impatience, she touched the bulging crust of clay surrounding the original entrance hole.

"So lonely," she insisted. "Please let it out."

Not quite sure of her meaning, he picked up a crowbar and tapped the hardened crust. This seemed to be what she desired, for she stood aside expectantly. Cracking the surface, he dislodged a section and allowed the gummy interior substance to flow out.

The girl smiled her pleasure, then cupped both hands over the soft mass, working them below the surface almost lovingly.

"So lonely," she murmured, in a crooning voice.

When she withdrew her hands, smeared with the gummy exudation, she held a small lump of some kind in her palms.

As she rubbed the clay away, Marlin saw with a start that it was a dead field mouse.

This was one of the numerous creatures that had been enmeshed in the sticky clay, he realized. But how had the girl known it was there—close to the surface at this point?

"Better throw it into the incinerator," he advised gently. "Nasty thing. Dead."

Shrinking from his outstretched hand, she cuddled the mire-covered little body to her breast and almost furtively escaped down the ladder.

She had cleaned the bedraggled little corpse and was still cuddling it happily, when Marlin descended to obtain his share of the meager rations. He was struck by the Madonna-like expression of the girl's features. Wonderful—the mother instinct—he reflected. Wonderful, yet sometimes pitiful.

DuChane stared as he took his packing-box seat at the table. "Where'd the kid get that?"

"Never you mind," bristled Maw.

"She can keep it if she wants to. What harm's it doing, I'd like to know?"

DuChane sniffed the air, as if in anticipation. "About this time tomorrow—if there is such a thing—you'll need no urging. If there's any stink more potent than an overripe rodent, I'd hate to find out about it."

"How does it happen," demanded Sally, "that the stuff out there didn't act the way it does when we throw things away?"

"That's a thought!" DuChane agreed. "Whatever we throwaway, the shell digests—tin cans, refuse, scraps. But this—" He shrugged. "Just one of those freakish accidents, I suppose."

THE strange aftermath was that when they gathered for another meal, after the usual sleep period, the mouse was standing on its tiny hind legs, daintily nibbling crumbs from Pearl's hand.

"This thing gets more uncanny," DuChane growled. "We were wondering how the stuff came to leave the creature intact. Now we find that it knows the difference between inert objects and those potentially alive. Not only that, but it seems to know how to keep the creatures in suspended animation."

"You talk as if the ship was something alive," observed Sally sharply.

"It's quite possible," Marlin suggested, "to conceive of chemicals in the clay which attack dead tissue, but to which live cells are resistant."

"Intelligent chemicals! That's a hot one!" retorted the girl.

Marlin eyed her calmly. "It's not so farfetched. I can name one chemical right off the bat—just plain water. Put dead vegetation in a damp spot and it decays. Live vegetation draws nourishment and thrives under the same condition."

McGruder eyed with distaste the slender rations set out before him, then glanced up longingly at the enclosing sphere.

"There must be a mess of them dead animals out in that clay. I wouldn't mind havin' a little fresh meat, even if it was only a chipmunk."

The suggestion was received apathetically, but Marlin found himself reflecting that this might offer a not impossible solution of their food problem—presuming that they survived the dwindling stock of canned provisions.

CHAPTER TWELVE

FOR the most part, the vessel had proceeded without producing any sense of motion. A violent shift would have dislodged everything loose in the shell—the scaffolding, ladders, the temporarily secured electric lights—and yet there had been nothing of the sort. Once in awhile, they felt a trembling jar. This probably was caused by the impact of a meteorite. But thus far, no such bodies had pierced the heavy insulation of resistant clay.

There was now, however, quite a definite indication that they were moving in space. Observations taken at intervals showed that the "moon" was coming closer. Presently, the irregularities on the edge of the disc were apparent to the eye, and shadowy configurations on its rocky surface could be discerned.

After some days, Marlin developed a new suspicion.

He checked his observations carefully. There was no doubt about it. They were no longer approaching the mass but were drifting in an orbit around it—either that, or it was rotating around the sphere. And about this time he made a further discovery. A second body had appeared in the heavens—and presently there was a third.

"There's only one explanation," he reported tersely at a mealtime gathering. "We're in the asteroid belt."

DuChane alone seemed to know what this meant.

"Dave seems to be jumping at conclusions, but assuming that he's right, we've swung out beyond the orbit of Mars— somewhere between it and Jupiter. There's a region of small planets, masses of rock, ranging up to four or five hundred miles in diameter. Supposed to be fragments of a planet that broke up somehow."

"Or didn't quite jell in the making," corrected Marlin. "I believe that's the modern scientific view. More than nine hundred of them have been charted though I've no doubt there must be innumerable smaller fragments."

"What's the chance of our gettin' through without bein' hit?" demanded McGruder.

"How should I know? As a matter of fact, I don't think we're on our way through. Looks as if we've established an orbit—at least around that big one."

"Anything we can do about it?"

Marlin regarded him impersonally.

"Nothing," he said. "Exactly nothing. We've no more control over our fate at present than we've had since we started."

Sally gave a mirthless laugh. "That makes it swell! All we've got to do is wait—and wait—and see what this old ball intends to do with us."

Pearl volunteered a remark, which, in its unexpectedness, caused them all to look at her.

"So many stones," she breathed. "Lonely stones."

DuChane leaped to his feet. "The girl knew!" he shouted. "She knew! We thought she was talking gibberish, but she was telling us where we'd wind up. Stones! Lonely stones! Asteroids!"

"Of course Pearl knows!" crowed Maw Barstow. "Didn't I tell you?"

Norma rarely took part in their discussions. She spoke now with bitter conviction. A flush of intensity lighted her wan features.

"It was all intended! I could feel it when I lay there in my stupor—just as if I was a part of it and knew where we were going and why. It's a soulless thing! We don't mean anything to it—not any more than grubs. This is only the beginning— it's going to be more and more terrible. We'll be ground to fragments—"

She closed her lips and stared shudderingly, as if into space.

McGruder eyed her with resentment. "It's a lot of hogwash," he asserted with hollow confidence.

THE nine days' wonder of it gradually became common place to the rest, but Marlin spent a greater share of his waking time at the observation post. The three moons were joined by more. There were presently a number of gleaming bodies revolving around the sphere, the count increasing almost at every revolution. At one time Marlin counted eighteen of fairly good size and no doubt several were out of range of the periscope.

The strangeness of it was slowly borne upon him.

"Why should these planetoids be revolving around us?" he questioned. "They're reputed to have eccentric orbits, but we seem to have barged in on a small system revolving around one common center. And the most cockeyed thing of all is that we're apparently that center."

There might be some other explanation, but the reasonable one seemed to be that the vessel was swinging through the vast planetoid belt, "picking up" stellar bodies as it approached them. Each rock concretion drawn into the ever growing system increased its mass attraction for other bodies, and thus the accumulation grew, like an immense snowball.

Theoretically, there was support for the assumption. The plates within the sphere exercised an attraction that approximated Earth gravity. Normally, the attraction of so small an object in space would have been slight, but thus augmented, it might act as a magnet, drawing much larger bodies out of their natural orbits.

"Still, if that's the case," he reasoned, "they'd keep drawing closer. They'd eventually crush our sphere by the very force of its own gravity."

His mind pictured a churning mass of mountainous and smaller rocks, rolling round and round each other in ever-narrowing orbits, crashing and grinding together, probably generating heat in the process, eventually fusing into a solid mass.

"Nice prospect," he reflected with a shudder. "Where'll we be when that takes place? Somewhere near the center, from all indications."

The prospect revealed through the periscope was awe-inspiring, but increasingly fearsome. For one exciting hour, Marlin watched while two planetoids collided and slowly ground each other to fragments. On another occasion, a huge mass lazily crossed his field of vision so close that he could discern great areas of what looked like ice, mingled with towering spires of rock. He could easily imagine himself looking down on a mountain glacier.

"Why not?" he reflected.

"There's no reason why there shouldn't be frozen water in this debris. Presumably the general mass is constituted of the same rock, minerals, and gases as the other planets, including Earth. Some of it could be frozen air—or its constituent gases—considering the absolute zero out there."

He recalled reading the contention of Halbfass that some earth hailstorms originate in outer space. The scientist had produced considerable data in support of his theory that such bombardments may be of stellar origin. There was the case of an iceberg twenty feet in diameter, reported from Dharwar, India, in 1838, and a still earlier case of a block of ice "as big as an elephant" which reputedly fell in the same region during the days of Tippoo Sahib.

Unless Marlin was mistaken there were celestial icebergs among the growing mass of planetary debris circling the sphere.

The picture he had envisioned of the planetoid bodies closing in on the sphere, with its augmented gravitation, had seemed at first fantastic. It was taking on more and more the aspect of grim, threatening reality.

Collisions between bodies in the surrounding space became more frequent as their orbits definitely spiraled inward. Once a fragment drifted so close that it almost seemed to graze the sphere. As Marlin tensed for the seemingly inevitable impact, it passed by. But on its return would it not be materially closer?

That particular fragment did not return. Perhaps it collided with another and was pulverized or deflected from its course. But the sphere might not escape so easily the next time.

Occasionally, his vision would be obscured by what seemed to be a cloud of dust. It was undoubtedly just that—a field of particles from the grinding and colliding of rock masses, settling toward the gravitational pull of the sphere. On another occasion, the obscuring cloud appeared to be sleet—a mass of iceberg fragments, or perhaps more tenuous gas in solidified form.

SINCE that one shuddering outburst, Norma had seemingly regained her self-control. She appeared only occasionally at meal times, tight-lipped, reserved. Often Marlin saw her standing on a secluded part of the superstructure, wrapped in her moody thoughts. She climbed one day to the observation platform beside him.

"What can you see through that thing?" she asked.

"Take a look," he invited. "It's terrifying, but inspiring too—when you reflect that mortal eyes never looked upon it before."

She studied the awesome prospect for a minute, then drew away, shivering as if with cold.

"Give it to me straight," she demanded. "What's the payoff? Here we are in a thin-shelled bubble floating through a tumble of jagged rocks and icebergs. They're drawing closer all the time, aren't they?"

He temporized. "My biggest worry right now is that the dust fragments, settling down on us, will bury the periscope head. That will be the last of our observations."

"I said give it to me straight," she retorted.

"All right. Your guess is as good as mine. Frankly, it looks like the end. But it looked like the end when we shot off into space. Somehow we've existed up to now." He spoke impersonally, trying to keep the sympathy he felt out of his voice: "Come to think, Norma, I'm puzzled—"

He stopped, but she finished for him.

"You can't understand why a person who's been through what I have should get the willies now. I'm not afraid of something I can fight, I'm not afraid of dying. It's eerie things you can't fight that get me. Hearing that girl Pearl talk gives me the creeps. She calls this a 'little world.' What does she mean?"

Marlin started. He had used the term himself; probably that was how it came to fall from Pearl's lips.

"I know what she means," Norma answered her own question vehemently. "It is a little world. I was a part of it, I tell you, while I lay there between life and death. I sensed things through its consciousness—if you can imagine such a thing. I knew what all of you were doing, just as if you were maggots crawling around inside of me. I had a feeling of what it was bound for—this grinding and crushing and churning in space. And we're no more to it than the mice and bugs that happened to get tired in the sticky clay while it was forming."

Marlin looked at her blankly. Despite her vehemence, she had herself under control—though at the cost of what effort he could only guess. The strange thing was that he himself had been subject to like fancies.

"Natural forces are—rather impersonal," he conceded.

"I hate natural forces! I hate this little world and everybody in it! Why did you help pull me back to life? I never wanted to live. I could have kicked off in a gunfight and had no beef. But here we're helpless like rats in a trap. Why don't we all kill ourselves and get it over with?"

Marlin shrugged. It was pleasanter talking to Pearl. Her unruffled poise almost amounted to the assurance that nothing could happen which particularly mattered.

ON her next visit, with Norma's outburst fresh in mind, he reverted to the subject Pearl had once inspired.

"That idea about the world having a consciousness of its own may not be altogether screwy," he told her. "It would explain a lot of things that we take for granted. As an entity, it might very logically take a hand in the involvement of beings in its sphere of influence. Our surface life—the flora and fauna, including man—no doubt play an essential part in its evolution. The Earth entity, with its natural forces—the winds, tides, changes of temperature, volcanic eruptions, and such like—could easily direct the spread of these forms.

"Come to think—that's just what it has been doing, from the dawn of life. The only question is whether it happened by intention. Of course, I'm too much of a reasoning creature to believe such rot."

He stopped, half-awaiting the echoed response, "Such rot," but it was not forthcoming. From a pocket in the girl's soiled dress where she kept her strangely revived pet, a pair of beady eyes looked out at him brightly.

"All right, maybe I shouldn't have said a reasoning creature, but a skeptical creature. After all, it's as unreasonable to disbelieve as to believe—when you have no proof either way. Well, let's assume that you're right."

"Pearlie is right," she assured him.

"H'mm. Maybe so. Well, assuming all this, I suppose the same entity could carry the process further and cause all the activities of so-called civilization. It could stir up the restlessness that sends explorers and colonists to distant parts of the globe. It could inspire persecutions, such as those that drove the Pilgrim fathers across the ocean. It could drive men through greed, lust of conquest—any number of urges. War—perhaps that's Nature's way of purging elements she wants to get rid of, or preparing for some new stage of development. Which brings the topic down to us."

He glanced at her, half expecting a response, but she merely smiled in her vaguely knowing way.

"We all seemed to be free agents," he went on, "but somehow we drifted toward old Eli's shelter—a bunch of misfits that weren't of any particular use in Earth's economy. What financiers not under some strange influence would have invested in Eli's wild theories? And that pit of encrusted mire where the old coot was led to build his sphere. Who knows what substances were brought together by what we call natural forces, and mixed into the right composition to protect us for this dash across space?"

The sphere gave a trembling lurch. Something had brushed its surface, but in his intensity he scarcely noticed.

"There are only two ways of looking at it," he declared, breathing heavily. "Either the whole thing was a freakish combination of accidents, or—it was consciously directed. I'm just sufficiently space-struck to entertain the possibility that it might be conscious purpose. What do you say, Pearl? Accident—or purpose?"

"Or purpose," she assured him dutifully.

He gave a short laugh. "That was hardly fair. I should have phrased it the other way around knowing your fondness for repeating last words."

CHAPTER THIRTEEN

MARLIN regretted afterward that he had not attempted to offer Norma some antidote for the moody thoughts on her visit to the observation point. He might have tried to put in words his own fatalistic point of view. Possibly would have helped to sustain her if only he had been less preoccupied—

But it was useless to regret, when they found the girl stretched out on her sleeping pallet with eyes rigidly staring upward.

They gathered in silence around the inert form. Death had been their constant companion from the start, but this was the first time it had shown its grim face.

Maw Barstow began a low wailing. Sally also wept. McGruder moistened his lips and looked furtively around, cowering slightly as he saw the eerie features of Link peering from the shadows above. DuChane stood stricken but expressionless. Pearl alone, of those who looked down at the still face was seemingly unmoved.

"I seen her pokin' around in the medicine cabinet," McGruder recalled. "She musta swallowed some kind a dope."

They searched through the cabinet, but there was no clue as to what the girl had taken. Several bottles contained drugs, which could have caused death.

"Oughta be given a decent burial," McGruder commented.

No move was made at the time to carry out his suggestion. The only burial possible was through the locks provided for eliminating waste products. The thought was abhorrent.

"She talked kind of wild about ending it all," gulped Sally. "Said she could almost hate me for being the one to save her for this. Gosh! I even came back at her with a wisecrack—something about its being a good idea. To end it all, I mean."

DuChane spoke for the first time. "Moody sort of kid," he commented hesitantly. "Didn't seem to have a real interest in life."

"You tried hard enough to give her one!" Sally retorted with pent-up bitterness. "Too bad she wouldn't tumble."

DuChane opened his lips as if to reply, swallowed, then, with a lingering glance at the dead girl, turned away.

Eli was not among the silent group. No one bothered to tell him that his passenger list had been reduced by one.

The event seemed to do something to the morale of the survivors—something beyond producing the inevitable shock that follows in the wake of death.

Marlin felt it keenly. Until now—though he had imagined himself to be impersonal and philosophical about the whole matter—he had been sustained by a feeling that they were being carried on this strange journey for a purpose. There had been Pearl's predictions and their apparent realization—the uncanny fortuitousness of natural forces, which had preserved them thus far. It had seemed to presage intention of some kind—suggesting that they bore charmed lives.

Now, it seemed, the charm was not inviolate. They were no longer the favorites of some mysterious destiny. One had been snuffed out—the others could be. There was no purpose back of it—none, at any rate, which concerned them. As Norma had said, they were like insects caught up in the mud-ball. It was merely by chance that any had survived thus far.

The question of what to do with the dead girl's body was settled by the decision to cremate it. The waste incinerator was electrically heated and connected with a lock, originally intended to open into space, through which ashes and solid residue could be forced into the clay outer coating.

Though Maw Barstow protested and wailed, she had no counter suggestion to offer. DuChane held aloof from the discussion, but when Marlin called on McGruder to pick up one end of the blanket-swathed figure, DuChane thrust himself between them and gathered the body in his arms.

"I'll take care of this," he said gruffly.

A sense of bleak desolation swept over Marlin, as he watched the other man, with his somber burden, slowly ascend the ramp toward the blackened door of the incinerator.

At this moment the blow struck.

The concussion was so terrific that it sent Marlin sprawling the full length of the ramp. He brought up against a hard surface, dazed and gasping, and lay inert for a period that might have been minutes, vaguely aware of the darkness, of shrieks, and the crash of falling bodies.

Painfully, at length, he picked himself up.

As the sphere continued to heave and vibrate from the impact, someone fell against him. Clutching arms caught at him and a voice—Sally's—sobbed convulsively in his ears.

He disengaged the clinging arms. "Cut it out!" he said gruffly. "We're still alive—I don't know why. Let's see if we can find any lights."

Half dragging the girl after him, he made his way to the storeroom. He remembered a drawer containing flashlights. Several were broken, but he located a couple in working order.

Above the general clamor, the howls of someone apparently in agony rose with monotonous regularity. With the aid of the flashlights, he stumbled toward the sound, Sally following. Overhead the girders groaned and clanked with metallic reverberations. Several of them must have been fractured.

By the feeble radiance of the torches, he located the source of the agonized howls. Above the level of the observation scaffold—now a mass of tumbled wreckage—the gummy substance of the outer coating was issuing inexorably through a rent in the shell. Trapped in the deluge was Slinky Link—his face distorted with animal-like terror, one free arm pawing helplessly at the engulfing tide.

Marlin hastily sought a way of reaching him, but before he could salvage a ladder the demented creature was beyond help. His howls abruptly ended in a gurgle as the eruption relentlessly closed over him.

Sally was suddenly very sick.

McGruder, and then DuChane stumbled toward the light.

"Wha—what happened?" came the befuddled question.

"We were struck, of course. Help me get Sally back to her bunk. The stuff—swallowed up Link. Where are the others?"

They found Pearl sitting in a corner with Maw's head in her lap. She was gently smoothing the older woman's brow, which bore an ugly welt. Maw was groaning, but apparently more in fright than pain.

MARLIN swept his flashlight over them, decided they were in need of no immediate attention. "Let's see whether we can restore he lights."

In the control room, they came upon Eli's body wedged between two ranks of coils, his head twisted in a ghastly fashion. He must have died instantly, his neck broken by the concussion.

Tentative efforts to restore electrical current were without avail. They located a few more undamaged flashlights and inspected the vessel.

The first assumption had been that the dent knocked in their hull by impact with the asteroid occurred at the point where Link had been overtaken by the flood. It became apparent however, that the blow had struck on the opposite side of the vessel, where a much greater inundation had occurred—was, in fact, still in process of spreading over the interior surface like a great blister.

Link must have been flung against the hull from the girders on which he was roosting. His body broke through the weakened shell, and once the ooze had him it closed over him with implacable greed.

The utter hopelessness of their position weighed on the three men like a pall.

Any lingering faith that they were protected by a special providence was shattered. Already, three of their number had proved that death could strike as aimlessly and without warning in the space vessel as elsewhere.

The ooze was working in through innumerable cracks in the rotten shell. From serving as their protection against the cold of outer space and the burning heat of the sun's rays, the covering had assumed the guise of a soulless monster, spreading its ravening tentacles to smother and devour them.

DuChane's memory of the concussion was vague. The dead girl's body, wrested from his arms, must have hurtled against the shell, breaking through and being swallowed up in the same manner as Link's.

"Probably better that way," he observed gruffly. "More like a human burial. Wonder if any of that hooch escaped."

There had been an unwritten law that the small stock of liquor among the stores should be preserved for emergencies. Surreptitious violations there might have been, particularly by Maw Barstow, but no open drinking. Marlin shrugged.

"I guess we all feel pretty shaky and exhausted," he acknowledged.

The bottled items in the larder had been packed to withstand shocks. While there was some breakage, most of the liquor had survived.

The three downed a couple of rounds in gloomy silence; then, with scarcely a word, they stumbled to their bunks.

CHAPTER FOURTEEN

MARLIN woke with a smothering sensation and a foreboding. Fumbling for his flashlight, he sought the others.

Maw Barstow was snoring stertoriously in her cubbyhole. Pearl, who should have occupied the pallet next to her, was gone. Sally, pale from the retching she had endured, was sleeping fitfully.

In the storeroom, he found DuChane, lying in a stupor beside an empty bottle. There were several empties, in fact. DuChane and McGruder must have returned to make a night of it. But McGruder was nowhere in sight.

With a grunt of distaste, Marlin turned his attention to the hull. It was progressively deteriorating. The blow had ruptured the corroded shell-plates in numerous places, and they were constantly giving way under the shifting stresses.

His thoughts returned to Pearl. Strange that he had not come across the girl. He made an unavailing search of the staterooms, storerooms, the control room, and all passages and aisles of the unsteady superstructure.

A taut feeling constricted his chest. She was so defenseless in her childish simplicity. She might have wandered out in the dark and fallen from anyone of a dozen or more points of danger he could imagine. Memory of the fate that had overtaken Link, and presumably Norma's body, caused him to shudder.

From searching the likely places, he fell to searching the unlikely ones. His flashlight beam unexpectedly picked up the two of them—Pearl and McGruder—in a segment between the outcurving hull and the end-wall of the cabin-like structure containing their sleeping compartments. The narrow crevice between the corner of the straight wall and the hull made it an almost inaccessible retreat.

In the brief glimpse Marlin caught before McGruder turned his startled, snarling face toward the flashlight, the whole story was apparent.

McGruder had pursued the girl and finally cornered her. She was struggling to escape from his grasp.

The man cringed away from the light. "Get outta here!" he yelled hoarsely. "This don't concern you."

"No?" Marlin spoke with deadly intensity. "Take your hands off that girl."

"Says who?"

"I've still got the gun, McGruder—and I don't mind admitting that I've itched all along for an excuse to use it on your carcass. Let go damn you!"

McGruder jerked the girl roughly around so that she offered a shield for his body.

"Come ahead—shoot!" he taunted.

Marlin pocketed his gun. "I'm coming after you."

The lower part of the crevice was so narrow to admit his body, but it widened out above, where the hull sloped away from the wall. Pearl could have squeezed through at the floor level, but McGruder must have had to inch himself up a couple of feet before he could follow her. Methodically, Marlin set out to do the same.

THE feat required both hands, and McGruder seized the opportunity, when Marlin had squirmed himself part way up, to release he girl and plunge toward him with clenched fist. Marlin saved himself from a paralyzing blow in the midriff by leaping backward.

He snatched for the gun, but before he could recover it, McGruder was well back inside, again using Pearl for a shield.

"Smart guy!" he yelled tauntingly. "Coming in, are you!"

This time, Marlin held his flashlight in one hand and the automatic in the other, training both on McGruder, while he slowly worked himself up the angle formed by he two walls by pressure of his outthrust knees and elbows.

McGruder, eyes glittering, backed away, still holding the bewildered girl before him. Slowly, keeping he gun and flashlight trained upon him, Marlin squeezed his bulk through the crevice.

The vessel gave one of its now frequent lurches, groaning with the strain on yielding hull and weakened girders. In that instant, Marlin felt a movement of the two steel walls as they spread apart. He would have fallen if he had not involuntarily spread his elbows and shoulders to maintain his position. The next instant, the walls closed in on him, crushing— crushing—squeezing the life out of his body.

Even in that agonized moment, a horrified gasp escaped his lips, at what was revealed by the stabbing ray of the flashlight.

The heaving side of the vessel tightened cruelly, then released him from its vice-like grip. Limp with pain, Marlin dropped heavily to the floor within the narrow enclosure.

He lay for a moment gasping for breath, neither knowing nor caring whether any bones were cracked. Then he gathered himself for a supreme effort. His body was one solid ache as tortured muscles strained to obey his will.

"Look!" he gasped hoarsely, flashlight pointing. "Look— behind—!"

McGruder, struggling dazedly to his feet with the girl still clutched in his embrace, swung around at the warning, but it was already too late. A great seam had opened in the hull directly behind him, and a mass of ooze was pouring in, like a surge of lava.

Caught off-balance, he stumbled and slipped on one knee in the encroaching tide. A bellow like that of a mired bull escaped his distorted lips. He was gripped tenaciously by the pitiless exudation. His eyes roved frantically. Then, as Marlin dragged himself partly erect, he saw McGruder do an incredible thing.

Desperately, the detective twisted himself half around, with the girl in his arms, and forced her into the viscous tide. She struggled in a faintly bewildered manner. Bracing himself against her body, he gained a leverage which enabled him to release, first one foot and then the other. As he stumbled free, the girl was engulfed, almost before she could cry out.

In that moment of horror, Marlin was conscious only of a consuming rage—a lust to kill that obliterated all else. Forgetful of the automatic, he dived toward McGruder, with hands that had suddenly become claws.

"Don't! Don't! We've got to squeeze out of here! Before it catches—"

McGruder's screaming protest was strangled as ruthless fingers closed around his windpipe.

When the smothering ooze closed over both heaving bodies, Marlin was scarcely aware, through the red fury of his demoniac rage that the end had come…

…"But, mother, the goddesses were all beautiful, were they not?"

"Yes, son, but Pi-Ruh-Al was the most beautiful."

"Then why do the carvings always show Sa-Hala-Lee with a face, while Pi-Ruh-Al has none? I would think—"

"Hush child! The beauty of Pi-Ruh-Al was so dazzling that no mortal might look upon it. Even the gods could scarce endure its splendor, and no sculptor has dared presume to represent her features.

Not so with Sa-Hala-Lee, who is the goddess of N'urthly beauty and constancy. A touching legend relates to the manner by which she was wooed by Mah-Gurru-Dah Lord of the East, patron of the forge. He was forced to wound her, sore unto death with a lightning bolt forged in his smithy before she yielded—but thereafter she remained loyal with a faithfulness beyond mortal understanding. Yea, though it is reputed that both Maha-Ra-Lin and Bar-Du-Chan sought her because of her siren-like allure, she repulsed them with scorn.

"Thus wrote the prophets of old: 'In the beginning was El-Leighi dweller in the sun, who looked upon the sea of space and saw that it was a void, barren of all things. And El-Leighi hurled forth his thunder bolt and created a sphere of matter within that void. And he cast his thunderbolts again and yet again until he had created many spheres, which circled slowly through the emptiness of space.

"El-Leighi looked upon his work, yet was not satisfied. Four of his bolts had formed spheres revolving so close to the sun that its ray scorched them with heat unbearable. Others—the mightiest bolts of all—formed planets immeasurably far away, lost in frigid coldness.

"'So once again El-Leighi gathered his forces and hurled a thunderbolt into space. And on that thunderbolt rode great beings— gods inferior only to El-Leighi himself—whom he commanded to create a world on which life might exist.

"'When the thunderbolt shattered, in a temperate region of space beyond the fourth planet, these gods fulfilled their destiny by gathering its fragments and out of them creating a new world…'"

CHAPTER FIFTEEN

FROM a narrow strip of shore that fringed a murky sea, sheer cliffs rose—black, beetling, forbidding. In one direction the rampart lost itself in the haze of a bleak horizon; in the other it merged into a rocky but sloping ascent.

The sea itself was of a muddy hue, reflecting feebly the rays of a sun, which seemed to begrudge what little warmth it spared. The sky, gray though nearly cloudless, seemed overcast with a dusty haze.

Where the sea washed into a narrow inlet at the foot of the last great promontory along the line of ramparts, a boulder—distinguished from others because it seemed grayer, smoother, more friable—contributed to the muddiness of the sea.

Each time the tide rose and the waters swept over it, they softened and dissolved some of its outer coating. As the tides receded, they left a blob of mud, which slowly hardened through exposure to the sun, only to soften and disintegrate a trifle more at the next return of the tide.

It was an irregular tide. Its surges occurred in unpredictable cycles and in varying degrees of intensity. On a few occasions its high level reached a mark far up the cliff; on others it forgot to recede for a time; and yet again it was such a feeble tide that it barely washed the base of the boulder, which was in reality a clod of hard-baked clay.

Now and again, after the tide receded, some furry object lay gasping in the sun, and presently scuttled toward the less precipitous stretch of shore. Or a bird fluttered to the rampart, or a cricket vented a dismal chirp and sought the damp underside of a rock. In a nearby cleft, a scattering of seeds had been caught in the backwash of tide and blades of grass clung tenaciously to a meager deposit of soil.

How long the sea had washed this blob of clay could only have been estimated by some observer who noted its size when it was first carried down to water level in a rock slide, and watched the progress of its disintegration. But there was no observer to note these things.

There came a day—a day like many another, cloudless, murky, cold—when it would have been apparent, had such an observer existed that imbedded within the blob of mud was a foreign object. It might have been a log, for all the amorphous outlines revealed. Whatever it was, the water continued to wash at intervals over the coating, and gradually carried it away. As this continued, the uncovered portions of whatever lay within gradually seemed to lose their gray, desiccated look.

And there came another day when the coating was gone, and after the tide had receded and the sun had poured its rays down with unusual warmth for some hours, a quiver ran through the outstretched object.

The tide returned. As it gently lapped the figure on the sands, some instinct of preservation stirred in that which had been nothing but a core of foreign matter in a blob of clay. It shivered slightly and squirmed to a higher position on the shore.

When the tide next returned, the creature, born of a mud clod was hunched in a sitting position, gazing with dull, uncomprehending eyes at the bleak prospect, which was coming into focus before it.

...Just when awareness of himself returned to Dave Marlin, he could not have told. There was a borderline phase in which a bewildered, naked creature stumbled along the rocky shore with only vague consciousness of self. Memories of the past mingled fantastically with the present. Impressions of an endless journey, of a huddled group within a shadowy interior, of black, star-studded vistas, were intertwined with breaking waves, a sense of chill discomfort, and a dull yearning toward the coppery disc that hung in the mist overhead.

GNAWING hunger in his vitals gradually thrust the present into dominance. He dropped down and drank thirstily of the lapping fresh water sea. This partly appeased the discomfort, but a grub, which he pounced upon a moment later, satisfied it more. Eagerly he set about finding other objects to still that ever-present hunger.

Instinctively the man had turned toward the less precipitous region. Grim and forbidding though it was, it bore some evidence of life—increasingly more evidences on the rocky hillocks that receded from the barren shore. There were clumps of grass and bushes, an occasional bird winging overhead and here and there glimpses of squirrels, chipmunk and other small animals.

A tawny streak flashed through the bush. At the squeal of its victim, Marlin dived toward the spot, frightened the creature from its kill and hungrily appropriated the squirrel. In the moment of satisfying his ravenous hunger with the warm bleeding flesh, he was troubled by no memories of the process to which flesh was subjected before eating in that shadowy former existence.

Somehow he lived, aimlessly wandering, sleeping, when darkness came, in the shelter of the moment, constantly alert for something to appease the gnawing within him. More frequently than not, he went hungry, for the region was sparse in its vegetation and meager in sentient life. He chewed on roots, eagerly pounced on insect larvae, now and then caught or killed with rocks some of the small animals and birds that his unceasing search flushed from cover.

It is doubtful whether he at any time thought clearly, "I am Dave Marlin, a man, who once lived on a planet called Earth." His mind was far behind his body in recovering from the paralysis of disuse.

A new excitement stirred him one day. Farther inland, a thin column of smoke was rising. Smoke! The ascending smudge wakened something within him. Smoke was connected with that former life. It meant the presence of his own kind!

He climbed toward it with frantic eagerness and presently looked down into a sheltered cleft of a valley. By his former standards it would have seemed a barren strip indeed, but in comparison with the terrain surrounding, it was an Eden.

Grass and scraggly bushes struggled for foothold on the hillsides. A brook trickled through the bottom and its banks revealed crude attempts at cultivation. Stunted growths that looked like corn stalks straggled across a narrow field. A gaunt heifer was tethered on one slope.

The smoke rose from a smoldering fire on a blackened area in front of the cave. In the mouth of the cave squatted a woman, clothed in a shapeless garment of skins, suckling a scrawny infant.

Incoherent choking sounds came from Marlin's throat as he descended upon this scene of domestic tranquility. At his approach, the woman glanced up, gave a shrill cry, and disappeared into the cave.

From a crevice beyond appeared a man, likewise clad in skins, brandishing a crooked stick. At sight of Marlin, he stopped in his tracks, then scampered toward the cave, turning at the entrance as if to make a last desperate stand.

Marlin came on with eager stride, but he stopped a few feet away and the two looked at each other.

THE cave dweller was undersized, bearded, and shaggy. His arms and legs protruded in ungainly fashion from the ill-fashioned skin garment. Something about the manner in which the sharp eyes gleamed at him through a tangle of overhanging hair struck a chord in Marlin's memory.

"You're—you're Link!" he said thickly. The words came with difficulty from unaccustomed lips. "Slinky Link! Remember? I'm Marlin."

The woman's head emerged cautiously from behind her man. The scarred lip again prompted Marlin's memory.

"Maw—Barstow!"

"What you want?" demanded Link. The words were thickly spoken, as if he, too, rarely used his speech organs.

Truly Marlin did not know what he wanted. Nothing, perhaps, beyond the association of his own kind. For the first time he realized that he was cold. He approached the smoldering embers and knelt over them, gratefully warming himself in the glow.

The other two eyed him resentfully, but when the sun sank low they prepared a frugal meal and grudgingly offered him a portion. He ate greedily of the hard, gritty cake of ground corn and morsel of half-cooked flesh; smacked his lips over the swallow or two of thin milk, which they allowed him to drink from a crudely formed earthen cup.

The urge to talk was strong within Marlin—to exchange views with these, perhaps the only members of his kind in all the region. But memories of the old life and speculations as to the manner of their arrival seemed to have little reality in the minds of the two. Maw was brooding and taciturn, wrapped in an animal-like concern for her scrawny infant. Link vaguely recalled that they had wandered until they came to this valley, where it was somehow easier to wrest an existence than on the outer slopes.

He had found two half-starved cattle, captured one, and Maw made him keep it alive for its milk. The other was a bull, but so far it had eluded his attempts at capture. He had learned to make fire, the primitive way, through striking certain kinds of rock together.

These were his preoccupations. He quickly tired of the conversation and crawled into the cave to sleep.

In the morning, there was less to eat. When Marlin sought to help himself to the fresh milking, Maw snatched the clay vessel and scuttled with it into the cave.

Link thrust a piece of stringy meat into Marlin's hands, then caught up his stick and brandished it threateningly.

"This is our place," he snarled. "You go."

Marlin crammed the partly cooked flesh into his mouth.

"Why?" he demanded.

"Eat too much," was the laconic response.

Marlin reflected on this. He had not eaten much, but the little tasted good, and he wanted to stay.

"Go," insisted Link, prodding with his stick. He added as at afterthought, "You're uncovered—don't look nice."

Marlin looked down at his sun-browned body. In that vaguely remembered former existence he had worn clothes. Now he was naked. The thought shamed him. Disconsolately, he turned and plodded away.

Thereafter, the recovery of his brain cells was more rapid. The old earth life still seemed incredibly remote—as detached as though it belonged to another person—but upon its vague memories he drew in order to create a more satisfying existence.

He fashioned crude cutting implements and spears by chipping stones and fitting them to handles made from tough growths of brush. He learned deft ways of making fire, and usually cooked his meat. He pieced together an abbreviated garment of skins. Each day he developed new adaptations to the harsh environment.

Usually, he was too tired to think of anything beyond the physical needs of the moment, but now and then, after a meal of unusual repletion, he lay on his back and gazed thoughtfully at the coppery sun, or at the two small moons which, with their uncoordinated orbits, created such eccentricity in the tides. Then he recalled incidents of the past, of the strange journey in the clay-covered sphere, and speculated as to the mystery of his coming to this bleak new world—of the manner of its creation.

WAKING one morning, he was startled to find that a fire had been built and there was an odor of scorching meat. Erect in one bound, he stared incredulously at the other man who was nonchalantly making free with his camp.

"Kinda surprised—eh?"

For a moment, Marlin did not know the longhaired, bearded, skinclad stranger. He peered uncertainly.

"You're—you're DuChane, aren't you?"

"The old maestro himself," grinned the other. "Came across your trail two days ago. Campfires—footprints. Nearly caught up with you last night, but the dark overtook me. Guess we're the sole survivors."

"No," Marlin told him. "Maw Barstow and Link—I ran across them back there." He waved an arm vaguely.

"Maw and Slinky Link!" DuChane laughed uproariously. "That's good. Is the little shrimp still balmy?"

Marlin scratched his head. "I'd forgotten that. Guess he got over it, in a way. They've got a kid and a cow. Kicked me out on my ear."

It was good to have companionship. Talking things over made things clearer. For one thing, he hadn't been able to understand at all how he came to be wandering over the face of this strange planet. "Last thing I remember was struggling with someone—and the ooze closing over. Then I found myself stumbling along this coastline."

DuChane stared. "Don't you know?"

He took Marlin down to a sheltered cove. "There's a type of clay formation—you get so you can spot it by the color—and where there's one chunk you'll usually find several. Look for them above the tide level. Most of those below that line have been dissolved away. Here's a sample."

He took the small lump of clay—it seemed as hard-baked as earthenware—and immersed it in a pool.

"It'll take some time. We might look for more."

In the end, they deposited several of the fragments in the pool, and late in the day small objects began drifting to the surface.

"The clay dissolves. Seems to be somewhat porous and the moisture seeps through to what's inside. Recognize this?" He fished in the pool and laid an inert insect on the bank.

"Cricket," observed Marlin. "I remember—" His thoughts reverted to a small creature that someone—he could not quite recall who—had resurrected from the sticky ooze back in that shadowy interior.

"This'll do the same," declared DuChane. "See. Its legs are twitching already. Here's something larger." He fished out a bedraggled bird.

"Then this is how it all came about?" queried Marlin. He swept the landscape with an inclusive gesture. "These birds—squirrels—Link's cow and the bull. You and I?"

"Sure thing. And the vegetation. The clay is rich in seeds. Everything that blew into that pit stuck." DuChane raked the surface of the water and held the gathered scum in his palm so that Marlin could see. "Seeds. Insects and larvae. Must have been washing out and drying and blowing over the land-scape—taking root—for years."

"How many?"

DuChane shrugged. "Your guess is as good as mine. I think we'll find that the shell broke up along this stretch of coastline and all the life of the planet is concentrated here. It must have commenced releasing the life it brought as soon as the water reached it."

"But before that—how long—? The clay is hard as rock!"

"Dave—that's something to think about. I've an idea it was terribly long. That earth of ours—for all we know man finished his evolution there—billions of our kind were born and died—while we lay in the chrysalis waiting for conditions to ripen. Worlds aren't finished in a day—unless you're thinking of cosmic days. Not even when it's a case of gathering up the debris of an asteroid belt and molding it into a planet—a New Earth."

Marlin stared. His mind sought to envision the slow natural processes that would achieve such a result.

"It's not hard to conceive," continued DuChane reflectively. "Earth scientists generally agreed that the original life spores reached our system from distant parts of the galaxy. When you think of the distances and eons of time they had to traverse, our little moment of suspended existence fades into insignificance."

"You've been awake—longer than I have," Marlin confessed dazedly. "My rusty brain can't follow you."

CHAPTER SIXTEEN

THEY wandered down the coastline, the two together faring better in the hunt for small game and edible growths than either had succeeded in doing alone.

Whenever he found a scattering of the baked clay fragments, or even isolated lumps, Marlin made it a point to carry them down to the water's edge, where in due course they would add to the life of the planet. It would be splendid to locate some larger pieces. There might be something to those stories of goats and sheep trapped by the ooze. A dog would be a find.

DuChane was off hunting by himself when Marlin came upon the largest deposit of clay fragments he had yet encountered. One of the lumps was of boulder size. He studied it with mounting excitement. It might prove entirely barren, as many of the fragments did, or it might prove to contain only tiny creatures. On the other hand, it could be the chrysalis of a fairly good-sized animal.

Transporting it to the water's edge was out of the question, but Marlin solved the problem by dredging a channel through the sand and rock debris, which had isolated the deposit. When the next tide rose, it poured through the channel, immersing the clay boulder, and when the tide receded, the greater part of the water remained in the pool.

He did not tell DuChane of his discovery when they returned to camp at sundown. It would be a thrill to surprise him, if the find proved worth while.

Beyond assuring himself at intervals that the clay boulder was covered with water, there was little that Marlin could do to assist nature. From morning to morning, on various pretexts, he opposed DuChane's restless desire to move camp, while he watched the slow disintegration of the clay. Now and then he fished small creatures out of the water; others floated to the edge and revived of themselves. He was beginning to fear that the large blob contained no more than a sprinkling of such life, when, peering through the murky water, he saw a streak of lighter coloration along one side.

That it might be a human limb he refused even to hope. It seemed hairless, but often the small animals were bald in spots when they emerged, presenting a pathetically moth-eaten appearance. He could do nothing all day but watch. At sundown, DuChane made caustic observations upon his failure to contribute to their larder. Marlin scarcely bothered to offer an excuse.

Early next morning, he was back at the pool. By this time, the body within the partly disintegrated chrysalis was so definitely outlined that he could almost be certain of its human shape. The exposed portions were still hard and rigid to the touch. He restrained his impatience to break away the encrusting clay. Experience had shown that attempts to hasten the process usually resulted in injury or death to the enclosed creature. Yet by mid-afternoon enough of the deposit had dissolved to assure Marlin, not only that the body was human, but that it was quite probably feminine. The head and upper portion were still encrusted with the clay. He could only hope that they would be free by morning.

Had it not been for questions it would arouse in DuChane's mind, he would have remained all night by the pool. When he forced himself to return to camp, DuChane regarded him sourly. Suspicion mounted as Marlin set about unaccustomed preparations.

SELECTING the sharpest of his stone implements, he ground it to a still keener edge. Then, painfully and methodically, he began scraping his beard. The coming of darkness made little difference, since he was working by sense of touch. When the growth had been removed from his face, after a fashion, he hacked at his tangled locks until something that might be termed a haircut had been achieved.

Long before he had finished, DuChane was snoring, but in the morning he looked at his companion with undisguised amusement.

"Why the beauty treatment?"

"We're civilized beings," retorted Marlin defensively. "Why look like savages?"

Restraining his impatience until he was sure DuChane had gone his own way, he gathered some food and all the animal skins they had accumulated between them and hastened to the pool.

A tide had risen and ebbed during the night, leaving the water comparatively clear. The body of the girl was floating on the surface, face and shoulders entirely freed of clay but submerged.

A desperate fear clutched Marlin's vitals. He should have been there when the last of the clay dissolved, ready to drag her clear of the water. What if the delay had allowed her to drown?

Dropping his armful of skins on a flattened rock, he plunged into the pool and bore her to the improvised couch. The skins with the softer fur he spread beneath, and with those remaining he covered the slender body.

Not until then did he look at the wan face with any impulse of curiosity. It had not especially mattered who she was. It was enough that she was a member of the human species—a girl.

Now he realized that she was Norma, the moody outlaw maiden. And with the realization came a stab of dismay.

Norma had been dead before the crash. The barest accident alone had saved her body from the incinerator. The life-maintaining clay had closed over her too late to preserve a vital spark already fled. No wonder she lay so inert and motionless.

With leaden heart, he looked down at the still features—so cold and immobile. Not until then did he realize how vehemently he had counted on bringing her into his world— how he had needed and yearned for such companionship. It had not seemed to matter who the girl was; but now he realized that he wanted Norma—that life would never be complete without her.

He touched the cheeks, the hands, the scarred neck. They were cold—cold as the stone on which she lay. And yet a sense of perplexity assailed him.

Not one fragment of inorganic life had been preserved in the clay, as far as he had discovered. It seemed to maintain all forms of life or potential life; other substances had invariably been consumed.

His clothing and everything he carried had succumbed to the disintegration, yet his body had emerged from its clay entombment unscathed—not only that, but strengthened, purified, adapted to its new environment, so that he experienced no great discomfort in a climate markedly colder than Earth's. He and DuChane had discussed this and decided that the body metabolism had been altered, making them definitely cold-blooded.

If the purifying clay could do this, could it not also have drawn the poison from Norma's system, maintaining a spark of life that still persisted despite her seeming death? From the mere fact that her body was preserved, what other conclusion was it possible to draw?

With renewed hope, Marlin set frantically about trying to establish respiration by artificial means. Was it imagination, or did he feel a slight surge of warmth in the limp body? As a last resort, he bent over the still face and blew his breath into the delicate nostrils.

A long drawn, quivering shudder swept the form. Stilling his excitement, he blew again and yet again, slowly working the arms back and forth. And presently, beyond doubt, she was breathing naturally, her flesh was taking on a glow of warmth, the long-lashed eyes opened for a second.

THROUGHOUT the morning, Marlin nursed his charge. From time to time, he moistened the pale lips with water and allowed a trickle to run into her mouth. When the sun reached its zenith, she made an effort as if to rise, and he helped her to a sitting posture.

She looked around blankly, scarce seeming to know what she saw, and aware of Marlin only as an object that moved.

She was not beautiful by Earth standards, but those standards were far away. To Marlin, her very presence was intoxicating. He could have knelt and worshipped her.

How long he had been observed, in his preoccupation, he had no way of knowing. When he glanced up at an overhanging rock-ledge above the pool, DuChane was regarding him with sardonic amusement.

"I figured you were up to something," the man called down. "So this was the inspiration for the shave."

Marlin licked his lips, stifling a wave of apprehension.

"She's mine," he said.

DuChane circled the ledge until he found a place to descend. Making his way down slowly, he strode toward the girl—would have touched her but for a warning gesture from Marlin.

He turned abruptly.

"We may as well get this settled." His voice was harsh—his eyes had grown hard. "One of us gets her—the other doesn't."

"She's mine," Marlin repeated doggedly. "I found her—opened the channel to the tide—brought her to life."

"You want her," returned DuChane, "because she's a woman. I want her because—she's the one. I'd come to feel that way about her back in the space ark."

Filled with a blind rage, Marlin plunged toward him. DuChane carried a spear, and he raised it in defense, but in the fury of his onslaught Marlin brushed it aside and heard it clatter on the rock.

He landed a fist squarely on the other's jaw and followed it with flailing blows on face and body.

DuChane made a quick recovery. He lowered his head and bored through the barrage to get a strangle hold on Marlin's neck.

Forced to adopt similar tactics, Marlin struggled for his opponent's throat. They fell together, thrashing over the rocky slope.

With an unexpected twist, DuChane wrenched free. Attempting to follow him, Marlin slipped on the wet rock and fell with a resounding splash into the pool. By the time he could scramble out, DuChane had recovered his spear and was warily bearing down upon him, the stone point poised for a deadly thrust.

Before the sure death presaged by the snarling features, Marlin cautiously retreated. By this time, his mind had regained its alertness. For all his rage, he realized that, unarmed, he was no match for DuChane while the latter possessed the spear.

Whirling suddenly, he made a dash for freedom. Before DuChane could hurl his shaft, he had scrambled over the edge of the embankment and was running toward camp.

Quickly, Marlin gathered all the spears belonging to their combined store. Thus fortified, he warily circled the higher ground that overlooked the pool.

DuChane was squatting before the girl, but his preoccupation was not so intent that he failed to glimpse the movement above. Instantly he was erect, spear in hand.

POISING his best shaft, Marlin flung it straight toward the other's breast. DuChane leaped aside, and the spear struck a rock behind him a glancing blow. The head shattered, while the shaft rebounded, striking the girl.

Sick with dismay, Marlin saw her recoil and then bewilderedly attempt to rise. DuChane caught her in his arms and forced her down on the bed of skins, then turned vindictively toward the man above.

Defeated for the moment, Marlin withdrew. He could not risk throwing more spears while DuChane remained near the girl.

Throughout the rest of the day, he stalked the other. DuChane was too wary to be taken off guard. He was even supplied with rations—the delicacies Marlin had brought from camp with which to feed the girl when she regained consciousness. He saw DuChane put occasional morsels into her mouth. She swallowed, mechanically but eagerly.

Toward evening, Marlin was sure he heard her utter a few hesitant syllables in answer to DuChane's low-voiced remarks.

He kept up the siege through the night, hoping to slip down unobserved and creep up on the other man, but the night happened to be one in which the moons were both in evidence. Their radiance was sufficient to give the alert DuChane warning of his approach.

The one thing to his advantage was an unusually high tide. It drove DuChane and his charge up the slope to a position beneath the overhanging ledge. Studying the situation by the first rays of the morning sun, Marlin decided on a plan of action.

He gained a vantage point as nearly as possible above the two. By hurling himself over the ledge, he might be able to overcome the other in a surprise attack.

Waiting until the murmur of voices below indicated that DuChane was at least partly off guard, he poised himself, spear in hand, then leaped.

It was a fall of a good twelve feet. He landed on all fours on the sloping descent, the jar breaking his hold on his spear. A sharp pain stabbed up one leg.

DuChane sprang to his feet, spear upraised, but Marlin charged toward him without hesitation.

The jagged point of the spear pierced his side, but he plowed on, forcing the other back up the slope by sheer fury of the onslaught.

Again they were at close grips, gouging, tearing, surging back and forth across the slope. Once DuChane gained a strangle hold on Marlin's throat. Fingers, hard and cruel as talons, sank deep into his windpipe. Mustering all his energy,

Marlin broke the hold by forcing the other back against the rock wall and pounding his head against the jagged surface.

They broke apart, Marlin gasping for breath, DuChane shaking his shaggy head to clear it. Then, with the fury of desperation, Marlin stumbled back to the fray.

This time DuChane met the attack by hurling his body down upon him with the force of a catapult.

They hurtled down the slope together, but Marlin was beneath, and the crash of landing knocked the breath from his body.

DuChane scrambled for his spear, but when Marlin tried to rise, he found his muscles too weak to obey the demand of his will. He was faint from loss of the blood, which gushed from his torn side, and the pain stabbing up from his ankle was rising to the threshold of consciousness with unbearable intensity.

With glazing eyes, he looked up to see DuChane poised for the kill.

The spear-arm hesitated. Through a throbbing haze of waning consciousness, Marlin heard the other man's voice.

"I don't want to kill you—Dave. What about it? Will you go your way and leave us in peace?"

Then blackness blotted out the scene.

CHAPTER SEVENTEEN

MARLIN regained consciousness in the camp. He was stiff and weak and sick with the pain of his ankle. DuChane and the girl stood over him.

"Sorry, old man," DuChane said regretfully. "You put up a good fight, but I had the advantage."

Marlin made no reply. But in the days that followed, while slowly regaining his strength, he observed the pair. It was clear that he was definitely out of the picture. The girl,

Norma, taciturn as ever, nevertheless followed DuChane with her eyes and seemed to dwell on his every word. Daily she accompanied him on the hunt, becoming as adept as a man with spear and club.

Sometimes she returned early to prepare the evening meal. On one such occasion Marlin abruptly asked:

"You like him? You're satisfied?"

The girl, in her single brief garment of skins, dropped down beside him. She was tanned and strong looking now, and a new radiance had replaced the old sullen look on her face.

"You found me, didn't you?" she said slowly. "It was you who gave me back to life—and I've never thanked you."

Marlin gingerly flexed his injured ankle. "Forget the thanks," he returned gruffly.

"It seems funny," she went on, "to thank you for saving me. I used to reproach you for saving me the first time, and I tried to fling away the life you'd given back. But somehow, now, it's different. I want to live! I feel somehow that I've found the place where I belong—a world where living is real and glorious, as it should be."

He looked at her thoughtfully.

"I guess you're right. Everything's as it should be."

As soon as he could walk with but a slight limp, he gathered up his spears and implements.

"I've a notion there's better hunting farther south," he observed.

DuChane avoided his eyes. Norma said nothing, but it was apparent that she wished to be alone with her man.

"I'll drop around sometimes—keep in touch with you," Marlin assured them cheerfully. "So long."

Thus casually, he set out alone in the wilderness.

FOR weeks he hunted along the shore of the murky sea. One day he picked up a shaft in which was bound a spearhead unlike any that either he or DuChane had fashioned. It was a crudely hammered thing of metal—and the red stain with which it was encrusted revealed that the metal was iron.

While he stood looking at it, a shrill vituperation startled his ears, and two figures came dashing over the ridge beyond. In the brief glimpse he had before the pursuer felled the one in advance, he was sure the victim was a woman.

She had fallen beneath the blow, but in an instant was on her feet, screaming, struggling, and scratching. Before the fury of her attack, the man retreated, and finally broke away, waving his spear ominously when she threatened to follow up the advantage.

Both became aware of Marlin at the same instant.

He walked toward them slowly. "Sally!" he called out, and then, doubtfully: "Len McGruder?"

Eyes riveted on Marlin's face, the girl approached, slowly, almost like one groping in the dark. She touched his cheeks diffidently with both hands.

"You're Dave! Dave Marlin!" she gasped.

McGruder eyed them with fierce resentment, then lunged forward and thrust Sally away.

"Damned slut!" he growled. "Get back to your brats."

She swung on him furiously. "Shut up! I'll stay where I please."

Marlin noticed with sickened comprehension that there was an ugly welt on her temple and many bruises showed on the exposed parts of her body. But then, there were scratches and welts on McGruder that might not have been due altogether to entanglement with brush.

"You'll stay with us tonight," Sally informed Marlin. "You'll be surprised at what a good housekeeper I am."

There was no second to the invitation from McGruder, but Marlin cheerfully accompanied them home.

Their refuge, like that of Maw and Link, was a cave. In an improvised enclosure, two naked children rolled contentedly in the dirt—one about two, the other a babe in the crawling stage. Cute little brats, Marlin thought, and Sally appeared to be casually proud of them.

There was no evidence that they had attempted to cultivate growing things, but they had a fire, and Marlin was interested in the forge McGruder grudgingly showed him. He had fashioned other things besides spearheads—crude knives and an attempt at an axe—but he jealously refused to divulge the location of his metal deposits.

As a special treat, Sally cooked a delectable stew of meat and edible roots.

During the evening, the pair staged a bitter quarrel over some trifle, in the course of which McGruder sent Sally reeling with a cuff on the side of the head and she came back tooth and nail to retaliate. Marlin refrained from taking a hand. The girl seemed able to take care of herself.

WHEN the embers of the fire burned low, Sally carried her offspring into the cave. McGruder, with a snarling remark that might have been taken for a goodnight followed her. Marlin made himself as comfortable as possible under a ledge some distance away.

He wakened at the sound of crunching sand. In an instant, Sally was beside him, her arms circling his neck. She was sobbing.

"Take me away, Dave!" she moaned. "I can't stand it. He beats me—he's a beast! It's been a living hell."

He stroked her hair gently, reveling in the soft tangle. He did not blame her for wanting to leave a brute like McGruder.

In point of fact, she was voicing a thought which he had been pondering as he fell asleep.

Her lips sought his and clung, deliciously.

"Your kids," he suggested presently. "You wouldn't want to leave them. How'll we manage—?"

"I've thought it all out," she told him breathlessly. "In the morning you'll start down the coast. If he thinks you're out of the way, he'll go hunting as usual. Then you can come back and we'll slip away together."

"Suppose he follows. With two children we can't travel very fast."

"What if he does! You're strong, Dave—and unafraid. I've always admired you. He found me wandering around alone, frightened and starved, and we—well, there just wasn't anybody else. You know how it is."

"Sure," he agreed. "I don't blame you, kid."

Another clinging kiss, and she slipped away.

Marlin lay contentedly thinking of the morrow. He'd found the companionship he craved, at last. Sally was an attractive kid. In this new world, for all its hardships, she had blossomed in a full-bosomed, satisfying way. Her kisses were pleasant to recall. Now he could establish a home and live the way a man was meant to live.

That she was already encumbered with two children did not disturb him in the least. Hungering for companionship, he liked the idea of having others dependent upon him— others for whom he could work and hunt, and to whom he would mean something.

True, they were another man's children. Presumably McGruder had some feeling for them; he couldn't be entirely lacking in human traits. Probably even cared for Sally in his way. But a scurvy brute who didn't know how to treat a woman deserved to have her run away with another man.

Involuntarily, Marlin strove to put the thought in different words. The idea of running away was repellent. Why do it by stealth? He wasn't afraid of McGruder.

Why not go up to him and say: "I'm making off with your wife and kids. What are you going to do about it?" That was better.

McGruder would put up a howl. Marlin hoped he'd be man enough to fight. Somehow, you didn't feel quite so mean about taking a man's possessions if you proved you were entitled to them by right of superior prowess.

But whether you took them by stealth or force, you'd have occasional moments of remorse. It wasn't as if—

Impatiently, Marlin twisted to his other side and tried to sleep. Thinking about it didn't help. Perhaps Sally's idea was better, after all. It wasn't the fight he wanted to avoid—it was the accusation he'd feel in the other man's eyes. Even a rat like McGruder could have moral right on his side...

CHAPTER EIGHTEEN

MORNING found Marlin many miles down the coast and still feverishly pushing on. Too bad he couldn't have left some word for Sally; but she'd probably understand.

His failing to show up for breakfast would be the tip-off. She'd realize that he must have decided that he couldn't do this thing.

In the long run, she'd be glad that the father of her children still had the responsibility of caring for them. What if he did beat her occasionally? Recollection of the fight they'd staged last evening recurred to mind, and he grinned. Sally gave as good as she took. He half suspected that she enjoyed the excitement.

Still, there were her kisses and her warm vital body. Most of all, there was the hunger for companionship. It was just as well to put a lot of distance between himself and these ever-tempting possibilities.

Perhaps, if he was doomed to be alone, he might find some creature of the wild for company. The section of the shore that he was approaching really promised well.

He had supposed that the center from which most of the vegetation sprang was somewhere in the neighborhood of his emergence. Probably just a fellow's egotistical way of regarding himself as the center of the universe. Now it began to look as if this region to the south was relatively a garden spot, the older section—so far as growth was concerned.

The bushes were more luxuriant; there were even some fledgling trees. Wild life was more abundant. He caught glimpses of rabbits and of a distant creature that might have been one of the legendary sheep, which were supposed to have been trapped in the ooze before the sphere took its plunge into space.

It seemed to Marlin that even the sun shone brighter; his skin felt a gentle warmth in place of the ever-present chill. It was almost like coming home.

More and more frequently he came upon things that gladdened his spirit. Sheep there undoubtedly were, back among those rocks, and stalks of corn, not nearly as stunted as those, which Link had painstakingly cultivated. Bees hummed around the blossoms of occasional flowers. At the base of a huge rock outcropping he found a nest hollowed out in a pocket of dry leaves, and in the nest were eggs—pullet eggs.

On the slope of a hillside rising from the other side of the rock was a small flock of clucking hens, scratching industriously under the supervision of a strutting cock. Off to the right a pair of goats raised their heads and blatted at him in mild astonishment.

A well-defined trail led to the crest of the outcropping. Trembling with anticipation of he knew not what, Marlin plodded up the path. Reaching the top, he paused. Something constricted his throat.

CALM and tranquil, like an aloof goddess, she sat on a boulder in a grassy knoll overlooking the vast, rippling sea. She wore a knee-length garment, which seemed to be woven of plaited grass. Her long golden hair hung in loose braids over her shoulders, and she cuddled a chick to her breast, cupping it in both hands while the mother hen; with the rest of her brood, clucked at her feet. On the slope above, a black and white pup paused in the act of worrying a stick, and stood looking at the newcomer with one ear comically cocked.

Marlin stared, entranced. He had no impulse to approach, but only to fill his eyes with the lovely picture she made—to feed his starved soul with the tranquility of her unconscious pose. Mature, brooding, poised—a veritable part of it she seemed—an expression of the universal mother-spirit.

When she glanced up from the fluffy thing cuddled in her hands, she seemed scarcely surprised at seeing him, but her full lips broke into a smile of pleased welcome.

As she deposited the fledgling on the ground among its mates, he took a diffident step toward her, then another.

"Pearl!" he muttered in a choked voice, and dropped on his knees beside her.

She looked down understandingly. Extending both hands, she clasped them behind his head and drew his face gently to the warm hollow where the chick had nestled.

"...*Thus N'urth came into being. But it was a fearsome planet—barren—devoid of life. Then the gods who had created it turned to Pi-Ruh-Al, the all-knowing, and besought her to make their creation more pleasing to the sight of El-Leighi.*

"For know you, my son, that so great was the wisdom of this lovely goddess that for long periods she sealed her lips in mercy, lest she reveal truths too vast for mind to comprehend. Yet was she also the most tender and understanding of the Great Beings.

"In her wisdom, Pi-Ruh-Al gathered a handful of soil from the barren planet, and breathed upon it, and moistened it in the sea. And she scattered the soil and it became seeds, which blossomed into grass and flowers and all things growing, so that N'urth was converted into a place of beauty riding upon the void.

"And again Pi-Ruh-Al gathered rock fragments, which she moistened in the sea and breathed upon and scattered abroad, and the rocks soon gave forth living things, so that the whole world teemed with birds and tiny creatures that crawl and fly and burrow, and with all animals that we know, from the least to great herds which feed upon the hillsides.

"With all of this the gods were pleased, but in time they again grew dissatisfied, they knew not why. And Pi-Ruh-Al smiled, for the cause of their sorrow was known to her even before they voiced it. So she removed the seal from her lips and told them they were grieved because none of their kind would enjoy the beauty of this world or remain to husband its teeming life, when they returned to their home in the sun. And she commanded them to people N'urth with beings in their own image—children of their loins, who should hold their heads high and walk erect with understanding, as befitted the mortal children of gods.

"And the Mighty Ones knew that Pi-Ruh-Al spoke wisdom, and they obeyed her command. And now, from their far-off home in the sun, they look out upon the fair planet which they formed and peopled with life, and declare that it is good."

"Is it not true, Mother, that our own race—my race—came from the greatest of these?"

"We believe it is true, son—and ever should. For it is said that from Maha-Ra-Lin and Pi-Ruh-Al descended our splendid race, which peoples nearly half the continents of N'urth. Yet it is but natural for the other races to think highly of those from whom they sprang. All were *gods—stupendous beings of high courage and noble aims, who rode the thunderbolt across the void, brought life from stones, and molded for us a world in which it is pleasant to dwell."*

THE END

If you've enjoyed this book, you will not want to miss these terrific titles…

ARMCHAIR SCI-FI & HORROR DOUBLE NOVELS, $12.95 each

D-11 **PERIL OF THE STARMEN** by Kris Neville
THE STRANGE INVASION by Murray Leinster

D-12 **THE STAR LORD** by Boyd Ellanby
CAPTIVES OF THE FLAME by Samuel R. Delaney

D-13 **MEN OF THE MORNING STAR** by Edmund Hamilton
PLANET FOR PLUNDER by Hal Clement and Sam Merwin, Jr.

D-14 **ICE CITY OF THE GORGON** by Chester S. Geier and Richard Shaver
WHEN THE WORLD TOTTERED by Lester Del Rey

D-15 **WORLDS WITHOUT END** by Clifford D. Simak
THE LAVENDER VINE OF DEATH by Don Wilcox

D-16 **SHADOW ON THE MOON** by Joe Gibson
ARMAGEDDON EARTH by Geoff St. Reynard

D-17 **THE GIRL WHO LOVED DEATH** by Paul W. Fairman
SLAVE PLANET by Laurence M. Janifer

D-18 **SECOND CHANCE** by J. F. Bone
MISSION TO A DISTANT STAR by Frank Belknap Long

D-19 **THE SYNDIC** by C. M. Kornbluth
FLIGHT TO FOREVER by Poul Anderson

D-20 **SOMEWHERE I'LL FIND YOU** by Milton Lesser
THE TIME ARMADA by Fox B. Holden

ARMCHAIR SCIENCE FICTION CLASSICS, $12.95 each

C-4 **CORPUS EARTHLING**
by Louis Charbonneau

C-5 **THE TIME DISSOLVER**
by Jerry Sohl

C-6 **WEST OF THE SUN**
by Edgar Pangborn

ARMCHAIR SCIENCE FICTION & HORROR GEMS SERIES, $12.95 each

G-1 **SCIENCE FICTION GEMS, Vol. One**
Isaac Asimov and others

G-2 **HORROR GEMS, Vol. One**
Carl Jacobi and others

If you've enjoyed this book, you will not want to miss these terrific titles...

ARMCHAIR SCI-FI, FANTASY, & HORROR DOUBLE NOVELS, $12.95 each

D-21   **EMPIRE OF EVIL** by Robert Arnette
         THE SIGN OF THE TIGER by Alan E. Nourse & J. A. Meyer

D-22   **OPERATION SQUARE PEG** by Frank Belknap Long
         ENCHANTRESS OF VENUS by Leigh Brackett

D-23   **THE LIFE WATCH** by Lester Del Rey
         CREATURES OF THE ABYSS by Murray Leinster

D-24   **LEGION OF LAZARUS** by Edmond Hamilton
         STAR HUNTER by Andre Norton

D-25   **EMPIRE OF WOMEN** by John Fletcher
         ONE OF OUR CITIES IS MISSING by Irving Cox

D-26   **THE WRONG SIDE OF PARADISE** by Raymond F. Jones
         THE INVOLUNTARY IMMORTALS by Rog Phillips

D-27   **EARTH QUARTER** by Damon Knight
         ENVOY TO NEW WORLDS by Keith Laumer

D-28   **SLAVES TO THE METAL HORDE** by Milton Lesser
         HUNTERS OUT OF TIME by Joseph E. Kelleam

D-29   **RX JUPITER SAVE US** by Ward Moore
         BEWARE THE USURPERS by Geoff St. Reynard

D-30   **SECRET OF THE SERPENT** by Don Wilcox
         CRUSADE ACROSS THE VOID by Dwight V. Swain

ARMCHAIR SCIENCE FICTION CLASSICS, $12.95 each

C-7   **THE SHAVER MYSTERY, Book One**
       by Richard S. Shaver

C-8   **THE SHAVER MYSTERY, Book Two**
       by Richard S. Shaver

C-9   **MURDER IN SPACE** by David V. Reed
       by David V. Reed

ARMCHAIR MASTERS OF SCIENCE FICTION SERIES, $16.95 each

M-3   **MASTERS OF SCIENCE FICTION, Vol. Three**
       Robert Sheckley, "The Perfect Woman" and other tales

M-4   **MASTERS OF SCIENCE FICTION, Vol. Four**
       Mack Reynolds, "Stowaway" and other tales

If you've enjoyed this book, you will not want to miss these terrific titles...

ARMCHAIR SCI-FI, FANTASY, & HORROR DOUBLE NOVELS, $12.95 each

D-41   **FULL CYCLE** by Clifford D. Simak
           IT WAS THE DAY OF THE ROBOT by Frank Belknap Long

D-42   **THIS CROWDED EARTH** by Robert Bloch
           REIGN OF THE TELEPUPPETS by Daniel Galouye

D-43   **THE CRISPIN AFFAIR** by Jack Sharkey
           THE RED HELL OF JUPITER by Paul Ernst

D-44   **PLANET OF DREAD** by Dwight V. Swain
           WE THE MACHINE by Gerald Vance

D-45   **THE STAR HUNTER** by Edmond Hamilton
           THE ALIEN by Raymond F. Jones

D-46   **WORLD OF IF** by Rog Phillips
           SLAVE RAIDERS FROM MERCURY by Don Wilcox

D-47   **THE ULTIMATE PERIL** by Robert Abernathy
           PLANET OF SHAME by Bruce Elliot

D-48   **THE FLYING EYES** by J. Hunter Holly
           SOME FABULOUS YONDER by Phillip Jose Farmer

D-49   **THE COSMIC BUNGLARS** by Geoff St. Reynard
           THE BUTTONED SKY by Geoff St. Reynard

D-50   **TYRANTS OF TIME** by Milton Lesser
           PARIAH PLANET by Murray Leinster

ARMCHAIR SCIENCE FICTION CLASSICS, $12.95 each

C-13   **SUNKEN WORLD**
           by Stanton A. Coblentz

C-14   **THE LAST VIAL**
           by Sam McClatchie, M. D.

C-15   **WE WHO SURVIVED (THE FIFTH ICE AGE)**
           by Sterling Noel

ARMCHAIR MASTERS OF SCIENCE FICTION SERIES, $16.95 each

MS-5   **MASTERS OF SCIENCE FICTION, Vol. Five**
           Winston K. Marks—Test Colony and other tales

MS-6   **MASTERS OF SCIENCE FICTION, Vol. Six**
           Fritz Leiber—Deadly Moon and other tales